Also by Clare Edge
Accidental Demons

MIXING
MAGIC

MIXING MAGICS

CLARE EDGE

HARPER
An Imprint of HarperCollinsPublishers

HarperCollins Children's Books, a division of HarperCollins
Publishers, 195 Broadway, New York, NY 10007

HarperCollins Publishers, Macken House, 39/40 Mayor Street
Upper, Dublin 1, D01 C9W8, Ireland

Mixing Magics
Copyright © 2025 by Clare Edge
All rights reserved. Manufactured in Harrisonburg, VA,
United States of America
No part of this book may be used or reproduced in any manner
whatsoever without written permission except in the case of brief
quotations embodied in critical articles and reviews. Without limiting
the exclusive rights of any author, contributor, or the publisher of
this publication, any unauthorized use of this publication to train
generative artificial intelligence (AI) technologies is expressly prohibited.
HarperCollins also exercises their rights under Article 4(3) of the
Digital Single Market Directive 2019/790 and expressly reserves this
publication from the text and data mining exception.
harpercollins.com

Library of Congress Control Number: 2025932751
ISBN 978-1-335-01386-6

Typography by Catherine Lee
25 26 27 28 29   LBC   5 4 3 2 1

First Edition

For my Patrick.
Thank you for letting me borrow
your name and share your life.
I choose you in every dimension.

Fin's Prophecy

The key is the story you tell yourself.
About who you are and who you may become.
Lives are stories.
Rooted in the telling, but also changed.
Clutched too tightly, stories cannot grow.
And grow they must.
And what story isn't made better for a bit of mystery?
Questions asked together, spoken aloud, or held silently in our hearts keep us connected.
Find your story—the thread only you can weave in the tapestry of magic. But it must be true. Only then will you find us. Only then will you bring her home.

PART ONE

Blood Moons and Sneaky Boyfriends Are a Messy Mix

CHAPTER ONE

the blood moon

I meant to conjure the demon. But I didn't mean for the Concealer to be *quite* so good at its job.

"Cai? Are you still there?" I hiss into the darkness.

The wind rustles through the leaves and something howls in the distance—distracting Clíodhna, my brand-new diabetes alert dog. But Cai doesn't answer.

Until he does.

"Is that a trick question?" he whispers.

"Well, if it was, you would have failed."

"So, I'm just supposed to ignore my girlfriend when she asks me a question?" he asks.

My stomach does a little flip at the world *girlfriend*. I like that Cai's my boyfriend, though I really don't know how I feel about that term. It's not itchy-wool-sweater bad; it's kinda pants-with-a-too-tight-waistband bad. I really like Cai, but I'm just not used to it yet. There's a lot I'm not used to. Being Cai's girlfriend (okay, it's not *that* bad), having diabetes (*absolutely* that bad), and not having Grandma Orla here for the Blood Moon ritual, or in this dimension at all (totally, completely, absolutely the very, *very* worst).

"Um, Ber?" Cai's voice is barely loud enough to cross the space between us.

"Don't go too far, okay?" I whisper. "The Concealer is doing a very good job and I don't want to lose you."

"I'm not going anywhere," Cai assures me. The emotion in his voice pinches something deep in my chest. It's only been a few weeks since my grandma disappeared into the demon dimension with our cat Darjeeling, an entire coven of rogue blood witches, and the Mystery demon I accidentally bound to me. I'm honestly surprised we didn't cancel this full moon gathering. But Mom thinks we need to keep up with rituals.

At least Clío seems excited. She circles me, her tail wagging furiously. It's her first coven gathering since she came home from the shelter with us a few days ago.

We've taken to calling her Clío, which is probably not an appropriate way to shorten the name of a very venerable (and slightly terrifying) figure of Irish mythology. But she seems to like it. Honestly, she seems to like most things. Another thing I'm very much *not* used to, since before her I've only ever had cats. And cats are pretty indifferent to everything. I think I understand cats better.

"Am I low?" I ask, holding out my hand, palm down so Clío can alert. Cai and I have taught her to bump her nose into the palm of my hand if my blood sugar is too low and bring her muzzle down on the top of my hand if I'm too high. Not high like that. High as in my blood sugar is too high. Because of diabetes.

Clío just wags her tail. Not low then, I guess. Or she's already forgotten the alerts. Cai worked on them with her for hours yesterday though, so I'm probably fine.

"Ber? Did Clío do her business?" my mom's voice calls through the darkness, making me jump.

"Yeah, almost done," I call back. I sneak one last look at the spot where the Concealer demon is hiding Cai, take a deep breath, and walk back toward Mom and most of the rest of the Bitterroot Coven. It's the first full moon since everything happened up on Flathead Lake, and we're gathered together at a secret bend in the Clark Fork River.

Mom doesn't know Cai's here. No one does. Well, except me. And Clío. And the cats, Frangi and Mars. So, all the animals know, but none of the people. And since Cai's the only mind mage present, he's the only one the cats could tell anyway.

Clío and Mars chase each other around my feet as I walk back toward the crackling fire, and I take in what's left of our coven. Okay, that's kind of a dramatic way to say that, but Grandma Orla is like the sun, and her not being here has left all of us without anything to revolve around. I'm honestly surprised Dutch Haemon didn't swoop in and try to take over. But he wouldn't stoop to attend a piddly little full moon ritual with us anyway.

Mom and Dad are closest to the fire, sipping something from a thermos. Mom's wearing a long red jacket, and her red hair looks almost as dark as blood in the light from the fire. Dad wears his usual jeans and a flannel. At least it's a red flannel. We're all wearing something red to celebrate the Blood Moon, which is also known as the Hunter's Moon. You'd think it would be a big deal for blood witches, but we keep it kind of low-key since the biggest holiday of the blood witch year is less than two weeks away.

Samhain.

It sounds like *sow-when*. It's the holiday called Halloween by geenin—nonmagic people. And I am determined to get Grandma Orla back to our dimension by then. Which is why I've conjured a secret Concealer demon and hidden Cai under a tree.

Coven gatherings are super private, like all blood witch magic. Cai and I would get in so much trouble if anyone realized he's here. But I can deal with trouble. And it's not like things could get much worse. Besides, Cai's here to gather intel. As a mind mage, he's sort of (almost) a human lie detector. And I think my family has been keeping secrets from me.

My sister, Maeve, waves me over to the other side of the fire. Maeve is three years older than me, a good six inches taller, and looks almost nothing like me and Mom. We're both soft, with round faces and big legs, big hips, and big red hair. Maeve is all angles and pin-straight dark brown hair that she's wearing braided into an elaborate crown. Her makeup is dramatic—smoky liner framing her bright green eyes. Her red dress is so dark it's practically black and it falls to her ankles, hovering just above her black combat boots. She looks exactly how you'd think a stylish teen witch would look, and she probably didn't even have to conjure a single demon to do it. I'm absolutely not jealous.

She's chatting quietly with Drew Haemon and the Vasquezes, Juan and Taylor, who make room in the small circle for me as I approach.

"Ber, how's the diabetes?" Taylor asks, and his husband, Juan, whacks him in the arm.

"You can't just ask someone how 'the diabetes' is,

Tay," Juan says, then turns to me. "I'm sorry about him."

"No worries," I say automatically.

"No, absolutely worries," Maeve says. "That's not cool."

Taylor holds his hands out in front of him.

"Sorry, sorry," he says. "I was just trying to ask how things were going. I haven't been getting very much sleep lately. The shop has been absolutely batty. It's our busy season."

"No worries," I say again. When Maeve glares at me, I add, "Diabetes always sucks, but it's a bit easier with Clío."

"Oh my goddess!" a voice squeaks in a pitch so high I'm surprised Clío isn't the only one who can hear it. I turn to see Francesca, Juan and Taylor's nine-year-old daughter. "She's so cute!"

"She's my diabetes alert dog," I explain as the younger girl reaches out to pet Clío's head.

"Wait, that means she shouldn't pet her, right?" Taylor asks, grabbing his daughter's hand before she can reach my dog.

"It means she needs to ask first," I explain. "She can smell my blood sugar, so she's working right now."

"Cool," Francesca says. "But I could maybe pet her later?" she asks in a smaller, hopeful voice.

"Absolutely," I say, and she beams.

"Was this the magical experiment you mentioned at the equinox gathering?" Juan asks.

"Um . . ." I glance at Maeve. I didn't really think through how to explain Clío to the rest of our coven. And I'd completely forgotten Grandma Orla had mentioned that we were going to attempt a magical experiment about my blood sugar. She didn't know that Maeve and I had already performed said experiment and I'd bound myself to a Mystery demon, and the rest of the coven *definitely* didn't know that. And they probably need to *keep* not knowing that.

"Yes!" Maeve says brightly. "Actually, do you think you could train cats to smell blood sugar?" she asks Drew. Her voice is all bright and I can tell she's trying to change the subject, and I appreciate it. "Once you get Thirteen Kittens up and running?"

The conversation shifts to the witch-cat breeding facility Drew is opening down the Bitterroot. Phew. Maeve's a genius.

"We're actually expecting our first litter any day now," Drew says.

"Can I have one?" Francesca asks, tugging at both of her dads' hands.

Maeve takes advantage of their distraction and pulls me aside.

7

"Okay, we definitely need to figure out how we explain Clío's training without mentioning Cai," she whispers. My eyes go wide and I wonder if she knows he's hidden nearby, but then I realize she just means in general. Our family might be getting better about trusting other magical people who aren't blood witches, but the rest of our coven is *not* ready for that.

"I mean, diabetes dogs exist," I whisper back. "That's what we told the school, that she's just a trained diabetes alert dog."

"Oh yeah, right. Cool." Maeve nods, but I can tell that keeping secrets is starting to weigh on her too. She squeezes her ceremonial dagger so tight her knuckles are white in the firelight.

"When we get Grandma Orla back, she'll help explain all of it," I say.

Mom starts to call the coven gathering officially to order, and I reach for my own ceremonial pin, which *should* be in a box in the pocket of my dress. But then I remember I lost it a few weeks ago and we haven't had the time or resources to make me a new one yet. Blood witches like us conjure by making intentional blood sacrifices. Usually this is just a little drop of blood from a finger. We have ceremonial pins and daggers that are kept super sharp, so they do minimal damage. Since September, I've just been using the lancet that's part of my blood sugar testing kit. Which normally seems totally fine, but as the other witches get their daggers ready, I feel a bit silly using my lancet. Even as I pull out the "Sir Ber" lady knight bag Maeve got me that I keep it in.

We spread out around the fire, forming a loose circle. The cats take their places at the cardinal directions: north, south, east, and west. With Dar in the demon dimension, Frangi is the most senior witch-cat, so she takes her place in the east. Closest to Ireland, and the source of our magic.

That thought sends my mind spiraling into a hundred questions—most of them directly related to Fin, the Mystery demon I accidentally conjured with my sister at the last full moon. The Mystery demon I miss for about a million different, complicated reasons. And the Mystery demon who said the source of our magic *was* Mystery demons, right before they disappeared back into the demon dimension, taking Grandma Orla and Dar with them.

It is our magic, our lives and stories that give you your powers in this dimension. That's what they said.

I shove the thought aside for later as Mom laughs loudly. I look up just in time to see her and Dad kiss. Maeve and I exchange a *can you believe our parents are like this* look. Well, it's actually an *aren't you glad our parents are like this?* look. They can be totally embarrassing, but they're also awesome.

They would be even more awesome if they'd stop pretending anything is normal or okay without Grandma Orla here.

But I don't have time to think about that right now either. Because then the ritual begins.

CHAPTER TWO

messy memories

"Thank you for gathering with us tonight," Mom says. "To honor the Blood Moon, we sacrifice a memory. Something we cherish. A beloved remembrance of a beloved. In this way we honor our ancestors."

Dad passes around scraps of paper as Maeve distributes quills.

"When we must rely on the memories of others, we maintain trust within our coven," Mom continues.

The idea is one I know well. The words are familiar, though it's strange to hear the phrase in Mom's voice instead of Grandma Orla's. And for the first time, I question whether or not it's true. I question my mom and our traditions. Which makes me feel like Maeve. She's the queen of questions. It's not like I just go along with everything, but things have always been more complicated for me than they are for her. I'm the one with extra power in my blood. I'm the one who is bigger than the world seems to want me to be. I'm the one with diabetes.

Maeve is the one whose blood isn't always powerful enough to conjure. The one who memorizes every spell and invents new ones when there isn't a good enough one already written. She's the one who is secretly dating a weather witch. And I look to her, expecting to see my own hesitancy on her thinner, older face. But her eyes are closed, paper and quill clutched in one hand, dagger in the other.

"Please, bring your chosen recollection to the forefront of your mind and linger in it one last time," Mom says, casting mugwort into the fire. The smell of sage fills my nostrils and Clío whines at my side. And she's right, this part of being a blood witch is really weird.

I thought I'd made up my mind. I knew this was coming. I knew I needed to pick a memory of Grandma Orla. Because she's my most beloved. But now, the idea of giving up any memory of her feels impossible. Which is why I have a few memories on deck. That I was supposed to have chosen between before now. Oh well. No time like the present.

Option A: The Aggregate Demon.

When she was thirteen, Maeve secretly conjured an Aggregate, though I think she was actually going for a Breed, which is a class B Multiply. I know she was as shocked as anyone that the spell worked. But that night, when Mom and Dad were on date night and Grandma Orla was distracted, Maeve conjured an Aggregate and let it loose in my room.

By the time Grandma Orla found me—because Maeve left me alone with the dang thing, even though I was only nine—I was sitting on the floor of my room with a slimy yellow sluglike demon the size of a loaf of bread that was churning out an ever-growing army of stuffed animals as I presented each of my snuggle friends to it in turn.

But as I let the memory play through my mind, I can tell it won't be enough. For the magic to work, the memory has to really cost you something. It has to be more than fun; it has to be deeply meaningful. So I let the next memory play through my mind.

Option B: My Diagnosis.

This is not a fun memory, and it wasn't a good day. But it wasn't a bad day either. Because we finally had an answer for why I was so sick, for why I'd lost so much weight and my mouth was so sticky. For why I had to pee all the time. Mom and Grandma Orla sat on either side of me, each holding one of my hands as the doctor told me. I could tell she'd told them first, and part of me was angry about that. I was almost thirteen, my birthday was only a few weeks away. Why didn't she think she could tell me at the same time?

But as the doctor explained what diabetes was, that it was never going away, that it was something called a chronic illness, I started to cry. I would have to give myself shots forever. Even when I got an insulin pump, if I ever did. That still had to be stabbed into me with a terrifying metal needle. But Grandma Orla had leaned over and whispered, "If anyone can handle this, it's you, my brave, brave Ber." And I stopped crying. Not because crying made me weak. Strong people cry all the time. But because she was right, I could handle it. I was going to have to. And I saw the fear in Mom's and Dad's eyes and I knew I needed to be brave and protect them from that. I wouldn't let them know how much it hurt. I wouldn't let them know how scared I was.

But I let Grandma Orla know. I let her be the safe place for my fear. And now she's gone.

A tear trickles down my face at the memory and I hear other witches' quills already scratching away, recording the pieces of their past they've chosen. But I can't let that one go. I just can't. So it's going to have to be . . .

Option C: Mayhem in Phys Ed.

This memory was only a few weeks ago, so it's fresh

in my mind, but also kind of muddy. Because my blood sugar was really, *really* low. I'd forgotten to eat the snack I shot insulin for because an accidental Tidy demon had snuck through when I'd injected. By the time I'd chased it through the school and found it in the boys' bathroom, my snack had disappeared from my brain as completely as this memory is about to.

Half an hour later I was low. Dangerously low. And I'd sneakily conjured a Messenger demon to tell Grandma Orla. She came just in time to stop the Havoc from destroying the gym. Because when I'd tested, I'd conjured another demon. One that could have hurt my classmates or my teacher. And I knew I was in so much trouble. But Grandma Orla had swooped in—literally. She was riding two epic demons and banished the Havoc without breaking a sweat. She was amazing. She is amazing.

Yep. This is the memory. I can feel the way it hurts in my chest but also makes me warm. I don't want to let it go, but I know I'll get Grandma Orla back soon and she can remind me of it.

"Everyone ready?" Mom asks.

"Not quite," I squeak as I scramble to scribble the shortest possible version of the memory down on my scrap of paper.

"Want to conjure our Dismembers together?" Maeve asks.

Dismembers are class D Memory demons, the kind we sacrifice memories to on certain moons and holidays. It's part of preserving the balance between the demon dimension and the mortal dimension. And when I pause to think about it—which I don't try to do too often—it is kind of violent. Ripping a memory away forever? I shudder.

Maeve's eyebrows are raised, still waiting to see if I want to share the spell. I almost say no, assure her I don't need her help. But then I wonder if she's asking as much for her sake as mine. So I nod. Besides, there's nothing saying we can't both feed our memories to the same Dismember. It'll just need to be a nice strong one.

"Together," I say, and as Maeve smiles, I can practically feel her relief. We hover our lancet and dagger over our chosen fingers (I've picked my ring finger on my left hand and Maeve's chosen her pointer finger), and it's kinda awkward, clutching the piece of paper between my other fingers as I brace myself to stab at just the right moment. I glance at Maeve one last time and then we take a deep breath and start the spell.

Letting go of thoughts so dear,
Dismember demon, now draw near.
Take this memory, as a gift,
Forgetting can be smooth and swift.

We prick our fingers on the final word of the spell and let the drops of blood fall onto the papers on which we've written our memories. The swirling cloud of red-and-purple vapor appears instantly. I still don't know if Dismembers move so fast that we can't see what they look like, or if they don't really have physical forms at all. Either way, we know what comes next. We each hold out our—now bloodstained—memory notes and the Dismember spins even faster as it absorbs them. And then the memory is gone. And so is the demon.

I look down at Clío, who is being extremely chill, all things considered, and then glance around at the other Dismembers as they whirl into, and then out of, our dimension. I wonder what everyone chose to forget, but my mind only hangs there for a moment because a shout echoes from the trees behind us. Right where I left Cai hidden by the Concealer.

But he's not hidden anymore. At least not all of him. He's running, chased by an entire flock of birds. And the Concealer must still be attached to his head, because it's invisible.

My boyfriend is running straight at the fire, screaming his invisible head off.

CHAPTER THREE

the headless boyfriend

The stream of curses that leaves Maeve's mouth is impressive. I think a few are even in Irish.

Juan and Taylor shove Francesca behind them, and Drew scoops his fluffy black cat, Lilith, into his arms.

Then I see Mom's dagger hovering over her finger as she mutters a spell under her breath.

"Stop, no!" I rush around the fire, tripping over Clío and only saved from falling into the fire by Dad grabbing the back of my jacket. "It's Cai!" I shout as I collapse on the ground, and Clío and Mars both climb onto my chest, determined to assess if I'm okay.

"It's me, Mr. and Mrs. Crowley," Cai shouts. "But, um, can someone get these dang birds to leave me alone?"

"You know the headless kid?" Drew asks.

"He's Ber's boyfriend," Maeve says.

"You let a geenin attend a blood witch ritual?" Taylor asks. His voice is a low growl and I don't know which will be worse: admitting Cai isn't geenin, or claiming that he is.

"Cai, get over here, I need to get the Concealer off your head," I say as I push myself off the ground. Mars manages to cling to my shoulder as I get up, his fluffy white tail making navigating in the flickering firelight harder than it needs to be.

"Wait, I'm still invisible?" Cai asks.

"Only your head," I mutter as I try to remember the spell to get rid of the Concealer. "Just stay still so I can banish it."

"Can we get rid of the birds first?" Cai swats around his invisible head.

The birds' wings glisten in the firelight, feathers shining as they dart around Cai. As I watch, I realize they're not attacking, they're just—

"Hold still," I say.

"But the birds—" Cai whines.

"Cai, just trust me and hold still."

He does, and the birds immediately find perches all over his body. A few even cling to the top of his invisible head. It's such a strange and uncanny visual, a headless boy covered in tiny, quivering birds. Cai looks like he'd be right at home in either a horror movie or some kind of hipster art installation. As Cai stands silent, headless, and covered in birds, the arguments happening around the fire find their way back to my ears.

"Drew, chill." Maeve's voice is harsh, harsher than I usually hear it with anyone other than our family.

"You know I don't believe a lot of the stuff my grandpa says about your family," Drew says. "But we heard what you said at equinox about other magics."

"And we've heard over and over again what all of you have to say about blood witch supremacy," Maeve snarls.

"It's not about supremacy," Drew argues. "It's about protecting our way of life."

"Do you even hear yourself?" Maeve demands.

"Is that boy geenin or not?" Taylor shouts.

"Keep your voice down," Mom says, her voice practically as loud.

I shouldn't have brought Cai. I know that. This is exactly what I was most worried would happen. Well, not *this* exactly. I never imagined he'd become some kind of parody of a creature from a spooky geenin movie. And I'm not sure if how ridiculous the situation is makes it better or worse or somehow a bit of both.

"Keys." Cai's voice is so low I almost don't hear it over the crackling fire and everyone else's arguments.

"What?" I step closer to him, reaching out my hand

and grasping his. However upset I am about this, I'm sure it's worse for him.

"They're all thinking about keys," Cai says. "The birds. All different kinds of keys, small keys, big keys—I didn't even know birds understood what keys do. Actually, I'm not sure they do understand what they do, but that's what they're all thinking about. Keys."

This information pokes at something in my brain, but I can't figure out what it is. It's like a key to a door, but I don't know *which* door. But I can tell there's something right in front of me that I'm supposed to be putting together, making sense of.

"Oh, gross," Cai says, pulling my mind back to him. "One of them just pooped on my head," he explains. "Which I'm guessing is still invisible?"

"Yeah, about that," I say. "I can banish the Concealer, but I think it's going to disrupt the birds."

"Sounds like a win-win to me," Cai says. "Banish away."

I gather some saliva in my mouth, imagining I'm sucking on something sour. I try not to think about the fact that I need to spit directly in Cai's face. Oh well. At least he won't look headless anymore. And it's an easy enough banishing, if I get it right.

Hidden well, you did your best,
Let him go, give it a rest.

And then I spit.

The banishing spell must work because Cai's head reappears. Full cheeks, dark eyes, floppy black hair, and a wide Cai smile splitting his face. Which is thankfully spit free. Though there is a large smear of what is unmistakably bird poo streaked down his left temple and cheek.

"I think it's time to get you kids home," Dad says, making me jump. I didn't realize he'd come up right behind me. I look past him to where Mom and Taylor are still arguing.

"Are we in trouble?" I ask.

"Oh, absolutely," Dad says. "But I think the priority is getting Cai out of here."

I scoop Clío up into my arms as Mars jumps to Dad's shoulders.

"It was worth it," Cai whispers so only I can hear.

"The keys?" I ask.

"Wait, what?" Cai frowns.

"The birds telling you about keys," I explain. "Is that why—"

But we're cut off when a class D Movement demon pops into the mortal dimension right in front of us. It's shiny and gray like the river stones it was conjured on. It has at least a dozen appendages. Some look like wings, others like . . . flippers? When it waddles even closer to the water, I grow more confident in the flipper hypothesis.

It's about the size and texture of a large seal. The demon's head is tiny, so tiny it looks almost ridiculous. Until you see the fangs. Which I'm very glad Cai can't (only blood witches can see demons). He's usually pretty levelheaded about all things demon-related, but convincing him to reach out a hand and place it on the demon's back might be a bit harder if he could see that its fangs are as long as its flippers.

"You're not staying?" I ask Dad as he bends over and places his hand next to Cai's.

"Oh, I'm coming with you," he says. "Your mom will sort things out with the rest of the coven and join us later."

Maeve, Cai, and I have to bunch together to all touch the Direct at the same time. Clío squirms in my arms a bit, and I can't blame her. Demon travel is strange and she's only been part of our family for a couple of days. The people at the Humane Society didn't know where she came from before, but I'm 99.99 percent sure it wasn't from a family of demon-conjuring blood witches.

The Direct's fur is soft, and I wish I could wrap my arms around it and try to go with it when it disappears from our dimension—back to the demon dimension, where Grandma Orla and Fin are doing who knows what. But it doesn't work like that, as my parents reminded me when Maeve and I tried grabbing on to the Domestic demon that had just finished the laundry last week as it disappeared.

"He's a mind mage?" I hear Taylor shout, just before the Direct demon zips us away from the river.

My stomach lurches as the demon deposits us in the backyard. Clío springs from my arms and races after Mars. My eyes fall on Grandma Orla's house first, dark and lonely and so, so quiet without her here. Our much larger two-and-a-half-story house is on the other side of the yard, blocking Grandma Orla's from the street. Hiding it. Just the way she likes it.

"Everybody inside," Dad says, shooing us up the steps, onto the porch, and into the house. "Do you want to call your mother, or should I?" he asks Cai as we all file into the kitchen.

Maeve flicks on the light and I'm blinded for a second, my vision adjusting just in time to see Mars spring onto the counter and then bound onto the top of the fridge. A move he couldn't pull off only a few weeks ago. Clío barks up at him, her very loud borks drowning out whatever Dad is saying to Maeve. By the time I get my dog under control, with a bit of Cai's help,

Maeve has disappeared up the stairs to her room and Dad is sitting on one of the kitchen stools, holding out his phone to Cai.

"I'll call her," he says. "Sorry, Mr. Crowley."

"I think it's my daughter who should be apologizing." Dad's eyebrows are raised so high his forehead is more wrinkle than not-wrinkle.

"Yeah . . . me too?" I offer. I expect Dad to laugh; he's the most easygoing of any of our family. But he doesn't. He crosses his arms over his chest as Cai sneaks past us, into the living room. I hear him talking to his mom, his voice too low to make out exactly what he's saying as Dad stares me down.

"I'm sorry," I grumble. "I don't really know what else you want me to say."

"I want you to tell me what the heck you were thinking, Bernadette."

Wow. My full name. Dad really is mad.

"I guess I wasn't?" I feel bad, I do. But I don't have an excuse. Not one he'll accept anyway. So I'm not sure what the point of trying to explain would be.

"That's even worse," Dad says, running a hand through his hair and tugging at it until it's standing up almost straight.

I don't like upsetting him. I don't like disappointing my family. But I'm kind of getting used to it. It feels like since I was diagnosed I keep discovering new and different ways to mess up our lives. But this time, I'm not even really sorry about it. And before I can stop myself, the truth is tumbling out of my mouth.

"Actually, I *was* thinking," I say. "About Grandma Orla. And I'm the only one in this family who still is. You guys don't even care about the message Fin left. Not really. Maeve tried to crack Fin's Prophecy for a couple weeks, but even she's given up."

"Ber, we haven't given up," Dad says. "We've just had other things to do."

"You *have* given up," I insist. "Don't pretend like you haven't. Cai's the only one who still cares. And that's why he was there tonight. To try to help me figure out what you've all been hiding from me."

"He was doing *what*?" Mom's voice is like a whip and I spin around. I didn't realize she was back. Obviously. It's one thing to say something like that to Dad, and another to say it to Dad with Mom standing right behind you.

The look on her face is so angry, so betrayed, and so, so disappointed. She looks so much like Grandma Orla that I can't even feel bad, the way I know I should. I'm just so angry and sad and hurt. So I cross my arms over my chest and stare her down. Which is probably a huge mistake, but in for an Annoyance, in for a Devilry, as Grandma Orla would say.

"We talked about this, Ber," Mom says after a long and deadly pause. "Cai's magic was to be used only to help you with your accidentals. He was to stay out of our heads."

"I have," Cai says, completely unhelpfully. "Like, until tonight," he adds, even more unhelpfully. For a smart guy, he really is an idiot sometimes.

"Cai, let's just—" Dad starts, but Cai keeps talking. I'm going to murder him if we make it out of this alive.

"She's trying to tell you your blood sugar is spiking," Cai says. "Clío is! Put out your hand, Ber."

I reach out my hand and my dog bumps her cute little snoot into the top of it. I'm high. I wonder how high. Maybe that explains part of why I can't seem to keep any of my very angry thoughts to myself even though I know fighting with my parents is not actually going to help anything. But sometimes it just *feels* like it's going to.

"You should test," Mom and Cai say at the same time. And something about them both looking after me is reassuring and completely infuriating. But at least it seems to kind of soften Mom toward Cai. And I'll take any win I can get right now. I pull my meter out just as the doorbell rings.

"We'll see you tomorrow, Cai," Dad says, ushering him out of the room. "If your mom is still willing to help us after your and Ber's hijinks tonight."

"Tomorrow?" I ask at the same time Cai says, "Oh, she totally will."

"Help us with what?" I ask, looking between Cai and Dad. But they disappear toward the front of the house without explaining.

"Test first," Mom says. "Then maybe I'll let you know what surprise we had planned for you tomorrow."

"Can I conjure when I test?" I ask. "I think it'll be easier than trying to focus my mind enough to *not* conjure."

"Let me handle the conjuring," Mom says. "You just test."

And so I do. Test. And let her handle the conjuring. When my meter says I'm at 284, I expect some level of sympathy from Mom. But I don't find it. She's just watching the Bitsy demon shrink the recycling down to the size of a baseball, my hopes for my parents actually helping us get Grandma Orla back shrinking right along with it.

CHAPTER FOUR
comparing notes

"So, did they tell you what the plan is for this afternoon?" Cai asks as we settle down at a table in our usual corner of the cafeteria. Cai sets his tray down as I pull out my prepacked lunch and I try not to be jealous of his stromboli. I don't even like stromboli that much. But Mom is still insisting on packing my lunches and including all my carb counts.

"No," I finally say, tearing my eyes away from the melty cheese and shoving one of the seven crackers from my lunch bag into my mouth. "But they said it wasn't canceled. So I guess your mom wasn't too mad?"

"Oh, she was mad," Cai says, shoving a huge bite of stromboli into his mouth. "And when your mom is a mind mage, she doesn't even really need to chew you out, she can just basically beam her disappointment into your head. And she took away my phone for the next couple days. Which is why I didn't text you back."

"Yikes," I say, dialing up my insulin based on the carb counts Mom wrote on the bags of food.

"Yeah, but, like, what about your parents? Are you in trouble?"

"I mean, they're not happy with me, but they said whatever we have planned is about my diabetes and, like . . . making it easier, I guess? And they said they weren't about to take away a super amazing opportunity just because I messed up 'big time.'" I put air quotes around the last two words.

"Okay, so—" Cai starts, but then realizes his mouth is too full to talk. I can see his eyes dancing as he chews and I know he's gonna totally spill the beans on the afternoon plans. Thank the goddess.

"My mom is going to help you get an insulin pump, basically," he says. "I don't fully understand how, but, like, that's the plan."

"Wait, really?" My heart jumps into my throat like a hope-filled balloon.

"Yeah," Cai says through the cheesy mouthful. Then he frowns. "Do you want a bite?" he asks.

"Cai, I told you to stay out of my head." I shove another cracker in my mouth.

"Hate to break it to you, but that one was written all over your face." He cuts off a particularly cheesy bite, making sure to avoid any ham. "Here, at least have one bite. It's like hardly any carbs, it's mostly melted cheese."

"Thanks." I take a bite and almost make a totally embarrassing and absolutely inappropriate sound as the cheese fills my mouth. So much better than crackers. And I don't want to be mean about Mom. And Dad. They've both been trying really hard to make things easy for me, which is what my pre-carb-counted lunches are supposed to do. But watching everyone else eat steaming cheese while you eat crackers and peanut butter should probably be included as some form of unethical torture forbidden by any reasonable society. Not that there's anything reasonable about middle school.

"So I was doing some research on insulin pumps last night once I realized that's what they have planned," Cai says. "And the patch pump ones seem cool, 'cuz, like, no tubes. But then you're kinda stuck with it on one part of your body. Literally." He laughs. His happiness is contagious. Not just because he's a mind mage, but because he's just kinda a happy guy. And it's been really cool how much he's thrown himself into helping me with diabetes the last few weeks.

Beyond just helping me focus my mind when I test and inject, he spends hours on YouTube watching doctors and diabetes influencers. I swear he knows more about diabetes than me by now.

"I've been watching some videos and I'm leaning toward the one with tubes that has the touch screen," I say. "If I get one," I add.

"Yeah, if." He winks. "Hey! Want to make a pros-cons list?"

"Absolutely not," I say. "But I don't mind if you make one," I add quickly. I don't want to squash his enthusiasm, but Cai and I absolutely do not make decisions the same way. He wants to weigh all the factors, get all the opinions, and then talk through it over and over and over again. And I love that for him. I really do. But sometimes I need to let myself figure out what I want and throw out a few of the variables that don't matter so much.

"Cool," he says. He's not at all put off by my lack of enthusiasm. That's the best part about Cai. He gets me. Maybe that has something to do with him being able to kind of, sort of, not quite, but almost read my mind. He swears it isn't like he can pull fully formed thoughts from my head, especially without permission. Which is a relief, because having him read my actual, unfiltered, totally random and often absolutely chaotic thoughts? I think that's more than I could handle. But thinking of his powers reminds me of the real question I have for him.

"We need to talk about last night," I say, shoving a couple more crackers into my mouth and chewing quickly. One of the really annoying things about diabetes is that no matter how distracted you get, you have to remember to eat once you've shot your insulin. I learned that the hard way once . . . didn't I? I try to remember, but can't. Odd.

"Ber?" Cai asks. "Last night?"

"Right, yes." I focus back on Cai, back on the task at hand. Back on the plan. "You said it was worth it, before we left the river. Does that mean you learned something from the memories my parents gave up?"

That was our theory. That something in the memories my parents would choose to give up might give us a clue into what they aren't telling us about why we haven't figured out how to get Grandma Orla back from the demon dimension.

"So I couldn't see their memories or anything," Cai says. I'm both relieved and disappointed. The thought of him being able to see our thoughts that clearly, especially from far away, is too weird. But it would have been useful. "But I was really focused on your mom's . . . vibes? That sounds weird, but not her thoughts, just, like, where her energy was going. She wasn't being evasive."

"What does that mean?" I ask.

"There's this energy people have when they're lying

or avoiding something," Cai says. My brain immediately snaps into hyperdrive and starts to wonder if it's possible to be boyfriend-girlfriend with someone who knows this kind of stuff, but I force myself to leave those "intrusive thoughts," as Maeve would call them, for another time and focus. "Basically, I don't think your parents are hiding anything from you," he says.

"And you think that's a good thing?"

"I mean, for clue gathering, no," he admits. "But for, like, having solid parents who want the best for you and aren't lying to you and, like, not helping bring your grandma back from the demon dimension when they could, yeah."

"I mean, I guess," I grumble as I shove another cracker into my mouth. It tastes like sand and I wish I didn't have to finish eating it. If only Clío could have come to school with me today so I could slip the rest of my lunch to her. But she hasn't technically gotten clearance.

"Um, Ber?" Cai asks, and when I look up at him, he won't fully meet my eyes.

"What?" I ask, suddenly very suspicious.

"Do you do this a lot?" he asks. "Give up your memories?" He finally meets my eyes, and I laugh at how serious he looks.

"Yeah," I say quickly. "I mean, only certain full moons.

And some major holidays. But it's not abnormal or anything. And not, like, *a lot* a lot."

"That seems like *a lot* a lot," he says, still way too serious.

I shake my head. "It's about collective memory," I explain.

"Seems like it's also about secrets," he mutters.

"Mind mages keep secrets too!" I hiss, trying to keep my voice down and barely succeeding.

"Whoa, Ber. It's okay," Cai says.

And I feel myself relax. But not because I'm actually relaxed.

"Stop that!" I snap. "That's exactly what I mean. You get all judgy about our traditions and you're over here like literally messing with people's heads."

A loud thunk startles both of us. When we look over, we see a bird on the ground. It just smacked right into the floor-to-ceiling window. Cai and I rush to get a better look at it.

It's big. Bigger than I thought. Bigger than the birds that clung to Cai last night at the ritual after chasing him out of hiding. And when it scrambles to its feet and looks back at us, I see it's a fluffy, scowling owl.

"Whoa," Cai whispers.

"I'm glad it's okay," I say, but he holds up a hand for me to be quiet and closes his eyes. After a long moment he shakes his head, opening his eyes in time to see the little owl rustle its golden-brown feathers and fly away.

"More keys?" I ask.

"What?" Cai's not looking at me, he's looking off into the distance, where the owl flew toward.

"Keys, like last night," I repeat. "Didn't you say the birds were all thinking about keys?"

"Yeah." His voice is distracted. "This one wasn't thinking about keys."

"What was it thinking about?" I ask.

"I don't know," Cai says, his voice barely audible.

The warning bell chimes, and we hurry back to our table to finish the end of our lunches.

"Wanna test really quick before lunch is over since we don't have another class together until the end of the day?" He smiles broadly. I want to ask him more about the owl, more about the birds last night, more about what the plan with his mom is after school, but we're out of time for any of it.

"Good call," I say instead, pulling out my meter.

I feel the moment Cai's magic slips into my mind. My thoughts are focused and clear. No background static or distractions at all. I put in the test strip, stab the fleshy bit under my pinky, and let the blood absorb into the stip.

Just a few weeks ago, when I didn't know Cai was a

mind mage and I was eating most of my lunches alone or on the periphery of a couple of friend groups I didn't actually belong to, testing my blood sugar would have meant accidentally conjuring a demon. But now, I feel a quiet, focused certainty as I watch the meter count down.

Five. Four. Three. Two. One.

Not a single demon. And a perfect 135. Maybe Mom has a point about the carb-counted lunches. My insulin-to-carb ratio seems to be working pretty well. I guess sometimes parents are right about some things. So annoying.

CHAPTER FIVE

deducti-whatevers

After school I discover that the plan isn't actually an insulin pump. Yet. But apparently there are a lot of steps involved in getting an insulin pump, and some definitely not legal but super cool mind magic can speed up the process considerably.

So now Cai's mom Greta, Mom, and I are sitting in one of those "Get Insurance Here" offices I've never paid much attention to before. And Greta is about to do some really cool magic.

"And who are you to the Crowley family, exactly?" the insurance lady asks, frowning slightly as she looks between Mom and Greta.

"You don't need to concern yourself with that," Greta says. Her voice is low and melodic, and even though I still can't feel magic—at least not the way Cai and Phoebe and Tempest talk about feeling magic—I know her words are carrying a demon-load of power.

"I just need you to listen to me very carefully, okay?" Greta places her hand on the desk and the poor geenin woman takes it. A rush of guilt floods my brain, but I try to remember what this will mean. Insulin pump. CGM. One step closer to this whole diabetes thing being easy. Well, maybe not easy. That's way too much to hope for. But I'll take easier. Even if it means letting a powerful mind mage mess around in some geenin insurance agent's head.

In the same low, musical voice, Cai's mom tells the lady how to click through her forms until somehow the Crowley family has something called Platinum Tier insurance. For free. Forever. The kind of insurance that means free insulin and no copays and deducti-whatevers.

I'm practically vibrating with excitement as we leave the office, and Mom calls my doctor to confirm our insurance and get me an insulin pump. But then I see the look on her face as she ends the call.

"What?" I ask. "What happened? Did it not work? Did the insurance thing not go through? Does it not cover—"

"No, no," Mom says. "Nothing like that. It's just that there's only the one endocrinologist in Missoula now, so it'll be a little while before they can get you in for the appointment."

"Oh." I try not to sound too disappointed. I'm happy overall. But I wince as I ask, "How long is a little while?"

"Well, the first appointment she offered was in February," Mom says, and I swear my head almost explodes. February? That's a million years from now. "But," Mom adds quickly, "she said they had a cancellation and we can get in tomorrow, but you may not be able to go home with a pump."

"But I might be able to?"

"I'm not sure," Mom says. "I just don't want you to get your hopes up too high."

"Too late," I say. "Hopes are higher than high. Higher than my blood sugar when I was diagnosed. Higher than—"

"Okay, okay," Mom says, laughing. "I'm just glad you're happy."

"So, so happy," I say. And I am. It feels like my chest might burst open and a swarm of happiness bees might explode and sting everyone else with happiness venom too. Which is a little dark, but hey, I'm a diabetic, my metaphors are a bit stabby sometimes.

"Seriously, Mrs. Anderson," I say, turning to Cai's mom. "Thank you so much. I know this was a really big deal and I promise I won't tell anyone and—"

"It was my idea, Ber," Greta says, cutting me off and placing a hand on my shoulder. "And I was happy to do it. But you're right, we shouldn't mention it to anyone. And I don't use magic like this lightly. If the system weren't so terribly rigged, I wouldn't have done it at all. But sometimes I think using magic to right the wrongs of unjust, flawed human systems is the right thing to do. Even if it's complicated."

"Thank you again," Mom says.

"Yeah, and—" I break off, my voice going all high and squeaky, and I have to swallow a few times before I can finish my thought. But I need to. "Just, thank you for not canceling this. Or deciding I wasn't ready even though Cai and I betrayed your trust."

Greta and Mom exchange a look and the swarm of happy bees in my chest suddenly feels less happy and more nervous.

"Ber," Mom says, and it's her serious voice.

Oh no. I shouldn't have said anything. I should have stopped talking after I thanked them. I'm always doing this. Saying too much. Being too much. But then she takes my hand in hers and squeezes it tight.

"I will never, *never* punish you by keeping you from anything that will make your life as a diabetic easier," Mom says. "Never. Do you understand me?"

I nod as tears fill my eyes.

"I never want to punish you at all, not really. But sometimes there are consequences for mistakes, for making really bad choices. And last night was a really bad choice."

"I know—" I start, but she shakes her head, cutting me off.

"I know you do, but you also don't. The last few months have been a lot, and the last few weeks have been more than any kid should have to handle. You and Cai have been through so much, and we're glad you have each other." I feel heat start to rise in my cheeks at the look Mom and Greta exchange, and I wonder what our moms think about us officially being a couple. Heck, I wonder what I think of it.

"But when it comes to anything to do with diabetes," Mom continues, "we will never ever keep anything from you that could make your life better. Not if we can help it. And today, with Greta's help, I think we could a little."

"But Cai is still grounded," Greta adds. "At least until the weekend."

"Fair," I say. "And seriously, thank you."

"You're welcome," Greta says. We all say goodbye and she gets in her car and drives away while Mom and I stand in the parking lot for a while longer.

"Mom, I'm so sorry—" I start.

"I know you are," she says. "And I think I know how you can start proving it."

Chores. Chores is how I can start showing my parents how sorry I am. I should have guessed. And not just chores, demon-free chores. At first, it's torture. Dusting is always annoying, but knowing you could just conjure a demon to do it makes it worse. But I practically have all Mom's and Grandma Orla's lectures about the privilege of conjuring demons for day-to-day assistance memorized, so I know not to even try to argue. And then, after a break to have a snack and play with Clío, I have an idea.

"I'm done with the living room," I say, sticking my head into Mom's office. She's hunched over her desk and barely looks up, so I forge ahead, trying to take advantage of her distraction. "I'm gonna go do Grandma Orla's study next." I keep my voice calm and super normal. No ulterior motives here. Just a helpful daughter who is making amends.

"Sounds good," Mom says.

Perfect. She can't even say I'm sneaking around now. Which I'm absolutely not about to do. I'm just going to dust Grandma Orla's study. And maybe also her bedroom. Possibly her hallway bookcases too. I'm being helpful.

Clío and I are out the back door and across the yard so fast you'd think we conjured a Direct. But when I get to the front door, I pause. Because Clío doesn't want to go in.

"Come on, girl," I say, stepping into Grandma Orla's kitchen and trying to coax my dog in to follow me. "This is home too," I explain. "Just like the other house. This one is where Grandma Orla lives, and soon she's going to be back."

Clío looks skeptical, her little doggy eyebrows drawn up in a way that reminds me so much of Fin. Who is not a dog. They are a demon. A Mystery demon. And powerful and dangerous and kind of the exact opposite of my sweet and lovely dog in a million ways. And goddess, do I miss them.

As Clío finally comes into the house, a feeling crashes over me that I think I've been hiding from for the last few weeks since Grandma Orla and Fin disappeared into the demon dimension.

It's not just Grandma Orla I miss. It's Fin.

And I knew that. Every time I have to stab myself to test my blood sugar, every time I have to risk an accidental demon coming through, it's a reminder that Fin could smell my blood sugar. That they could do so much more than Clío can, even though she's doing such a good job and trying her best. But I miss more than just

Fin's blood-sugar-sniffing abilities. I miss *them*. Which feels like a betrayal of Grandma Orla. I betrayed her to conjure Fin in the first place. I betrayed her when I let her go back to the demon dimension with them. And now I'm betraying her all over again by snooping in her house and *missing* a Mystery demon. Suddenly my plan to clean and sneaky-snoop around Grandma Orla's house feels like an emotional minefield.

"Okay, Clío, maybe you were right," I say. "Maybe we shouldn't be in here at all. Maybe it's better to just shove your feelings down into a little box and not look at them. Today. Or maybe ever." And of course now that I've decided to give up on this little adventure, Clío finally decides she's actually not scared of Grandma Orla's house at all and races down the hall, then disappears from sight.

CHAPTER SIX

melting clues and learning curves

I follow Clío into Grandma Orla's study. I'm still not used to how different it looks without all her demons. She stashes demons everywhere. Or she used to, when she was here, in this dimension, where she belongs.

A demon isn't released back to the demon dimension until it has fulfilled the narrative purpose of its conjuring. And to have that purpose last for days, weeks, even years? That's rare. Grandma Orla is super powerful. She had Defenders on all her special stuff, Minimizers for her clothes when she packed for trips. And you have to be one *powerful* witch to trust a class D Minimizer demon to last for a whole flight when it's tucked away in a checked bag.

Concealer demons used to hide half the books, keeping them away from prying eyes. And prying hands. Basically from me and Maeve, though mostly Maeve. I know Maeve has been raiding Grandma Orla's library since she's been gone, and I thought that would help us as we tried to decipher Fin's Prophecy. But I'm starting to think Maeve doesn't actually want Grandma Orla to come back. Which is mean and unfair, but sometimes my brain thinks mean and unfair things even when I would rather it didn't.

As Clío hops onto the small couch and snuggles up in a blanket, my eyes scan the room for clues. But I don't even know what I should be looking for. Even though the room looks different without the usual demons (and without Grandma Orla), I don't know where to begin. I sit on the couch next to Clío and let her rest her head on my lap as I search my brain.

The key is the story you tell yourself.

Fin left a message in Cai's mind before they disappeared, and I've started to think of it as Fin's Prophecy. I have it memorized at this point, but no matter how many times I've let the words play through my head, they never make any more sense.

"The key is the story you tell yourself," I mutter as I scratch Clío's ears. "The key is—wait!" My heart races as something clicks into place, almost like a key in a lock. A key. "The key is the story you tell yourself," I say again, my voice stronger, louder. Clío gives me an annoyed look as I dislodge her head and pull out my phone to call Cai.

But he doesn't answer. I call three times in a row, but it just goes to voicemail.

I switch gears and text him.

> I think I figured it out! Well, not all of it, but part of it. What if the birds are a message? They were thinking of keys, right?? What if it's a message? From Grandma Orla? Or Fin? Or both of them! The key is the story you tell yourself. Key. The birds were thinking of keys! It's a clue. I know it. It has to be. What did the owl tell you? The one that hit the window.

My hands are shaking as I press send.

"Come on, girl," I say, jumping up from the couch. "Let's go tell them what we figured out!"

Clío just stares at me and burrows further into the blanket.

"I can't leave you here," I say. "Grandma Orla doesn't even let Mars come in here by himself. Come on!"

I swear my dog actually rolls her eyes as she hops down and lets me lead us back to the main house. It's cold outside, way colder than when we crossed the yard only a few minutes ago. I hadn't realized it was almost dark. Maybe we sat on Grandma Orla's couch longer than I realized. I slip off my shoes at the back door as Clío runs into the kitchen. But when I join her, I find the rest of my family chatting away, cooking dinner. And they're happy. Which should be a good thing, right? I think of what Cai said at lunch, that Mom and Dad aren't hiding anything from me about Grandma Orla. At least not that he can sense. But if they're not hiding anything and they're just happily making dinner, does that mean they're actually glad she's gone?

Suddenly my need to tell my family about the clue I've discovered melts like ice cream left out on the counter overnight. It's still technically ice cream, but if you handed it to someone they'd probably be kinda bummed. And I don't want to hand my family melted ice cream. Especially not when they keep treating my need to save Grandma Orla like an Annoyance demon that needs banishing.

No. I'll wait to tell them. I'll wait until Cai and I have proof. Until we know exactly what message Fin and Grandma Orla are sending. Then they'll have to believe me. And then we can bring her home.

The appointment the next day is at seven. In the morning. Which is way too early to learn anything. Especially things as important as how your new loaner insulin pump works. I'll have this one, which is exactly the same as the one that's on order, for a few weeks while our fancy new insurance does its thing.

This is kind of like a practice pump. But with very real insulin. So I'm sitting as still as I can, trying to take in everything the diabetes doctor is saying. She's not an endocrinologist, which is the type of doctor who does diabetes stuff. She's a diabetes educator. So maybe she's not even a doctor. But she knows a lot. And it seems like she expects me and Mom and Dad and Maeve to all learn it. And fast.

"There's definitely a learning curve," the woman laughs as she gently takes the vial of insulin and giant needle from me.

Why are there so many steps to filling this thing up? The thought of having to do it every two or three days is almost as bad as injections. Almost.

Putting in the site where the pump will attach to my skin is somehow both better and worse than just poking myself with the tiny pen needles. There's so much plastic involved. Plastic covered in plastic, wrapped in more plastic. But in the center of all that plastic is a needle, a spring-loaded needle that shoots yet another little piece of plastic into my skin. It's called a cannula. And at this point, I think if I have to learn one more term for something to do with this stupid disease I'm going to cry or scream. Or, more likely, just suck it up and deal with it. Because what other choice do I have?

I'd imagined today as a huge celebration. The moment I finally got this amazing thing that would make at least some aspect of my more and more complicated life easier. But instead, it's mostly just overwhelming. And by the time I'm learning how to stab the CGM sensor into my skin with yet another intimidating hunk of plastic hiding *another* needle . . . I'm tapped out.

And stabbed out.

And worn out.

But at least all my new plastic parts are now attached in places they should be. My pump is shiny and black and about the size of a large matchbook, but metal is way heavier than I expected. It's in a purple case that I have clipped to the top of my leggings and attached to my stomach by a tube that's twenty inches long. Which seems somehow both way too long and way too short. The other side of my stomach now sports a little plastic sensor that still kinda hurts.

"Are you sure you want to go to school today?" Mom asks as we pile into the car.

"I'm fine with skipping," Maeve says.

"Irrelevant," Mom says, turning to me. "That was a lot of learning. If you want to come home with me instead, that's okay."

"No," I say quickly. "I mean, yes. I mean, I'm fine going to school. Really!"

I don't actually want to go to school. Not really. My brain feels like scrambled eggs and my stomach feels even more like a pincushion than usual. But I want to see Cai. I need to see Cai. He hasn't responded to my text from last night.

But he's not in Bio. Or at lunch. He doesn't show up the whole day and still doesn't respond to my text. I almost ask Mom about it when she picks me up after school, to see if Greta said anything about them going out of town or on some mind mage holiday I don't know about. But she just has a hundred questions about how things went with my pump. Which is fine. They went fine. It's really cool, and on any other day, I'd probably be bubbling with excitement about it and ready to tell her everything, but I can't shake the feeling something's wrong. Well, more than just my grandma being stuck in another dimension and me having an incurable disease.

"Ber, are you sure you're okay?" Mom asks. "If you don't like the pump, you don't have to use it. You can use the CGM without it. Or we can try a different one. I don't think everything is finalized—"

"No, I like it," I say quickly. "I'm just really worn out. Maybe you were right about school after the doctor's office."

"Hard day?"

"Cai wasn't there," I say, and then immediately feel weird about it, so I decide to just double down. "Do you know where he was? Did Greta say anything?"

Mom's silent for a long time, and when I look at her, I can tell she's trying to decide whether to say something or not. She's got her lips pulled in and her nostrils flare a little too much as she takes a deep breath.

"I think Cai should tell you himself," she finally says. Well, that's ominous. And now I'm full panicking.

"Wait, tell me what?" I ask. "He's not responding to my texts. Is he okay?"

"Oh, Ber, yes, he's fine," Mom says quickly. "But he should be the one to tell you why he wasn't at school today, if he wants to."

"Oh, okay," I say. And the rest of the drive home passes in a silence as uncomfortable as shoes three sizes too small. With heels.

CHAPTER SEVEN

a very special kind of disappointing

"Hey Ber."

I look up to see Ms. Abdullah, the Phys Ed teacher, staring down at me. Her hijab is black and shiny and reminds me of Fin's eyes as it reflects the fluorescent lights of the cafeteria.

"Oh, hi, Ms. Abdullah. What's up?"

"I was wondering if you wanted to join the diabetic kids' lunch," she says. "Or the kids with diabetes lunch? Sorry, I'm trying to use the right words."

"I don't mind diabetic," I say with a shrug. "I mean, I am one."

"Too true. Well, they have diet soda for you guys. Girls. Kids."

This is so awkward. It's always so cringe when teachers try too hard.

"Yeah, I'm actually waiting for Cai," I say, hoping she'll take the hint. It's not that I don't like Ms. Abdullah. As far as teachers go, she's great.

"Oh, you are?" she asks, and her eyebrows shoot up and her mouth pinches into a little smile and I know I need to do anything to escape *this* social interaction.

"Yeah, but you're right. It would be good for me to meet the other diabetic kids," I say quickly. "Which table?"

"By the salad bar," Ms. Abdullah says. "Here, I can show you."

"I'll find it," I say. "Thanks!" And I set off toward the salad bar.

The diabetic kids' lunch happens every Friday. I don't know why I've never joined before. It's not like they could be *that* intimidating. There are only a few other diabetic kids who go to Fort Missoula Middle School. And if the last few weeks have taught me anything, it's that it's important to have people who understand you. I haven't ever met any other diabetics (that I know of). Maybe Cai still being out of school and *still* not answering my texts is a sign I need to diversify my friend group a smidge.

I finally spot the table; the six-pack of untouched off-brand diet cola gives it away. But there aren't five kids there. There's just one.

"Who are you?" The girl frowning at me has long

blond hair that is perfectly curled. Seriously, not a single strand is out of place. She's thin and wearing a tight pink shirt and white jeans and all of her jewelry is the exact same shade of rose gold.

She looks fancy and I feel like a total slob in my old leggings and cozy red sweatshirt. Then I kick myself mentally because Grandma Orla got me this sweatshirt in Ireland. It's even got Celtic designs on the hem and sleeves. I was wearing it the last time I saw her. I wore this sweatshirt to feel like myself and I'm not going to let some preppy girl's perfect hair and flawless eyeliner mess with that.

"I'm Ber," I say. "Bernadette. Crowley."

"And you're diabetic?" She frowns again. What's with the skepticism?

"Um, yeah," I say as I settle onto the bench across from her. "I was diagnosed in July." I pull out my pump. "I just got my pump this week."

"Pump?" She frowns at my pump as I awkwardly clip it back onto the top of my leggings. "Oh, I just thought maybe you were type two because . . ."

She trails off and I can feel my face go red. I know why she's saying it. Because I'm chubby. Because I'm not thin like she is. My ears are pounding, and I don't know what to say. So I pull my lunch out of my bag and grab one of the diet sodas sitting on the table.

"You know aspartame is a carcinogen, right?" The girl raises her eyebrows.

And I almost get up. I almost take my soda and walk across the lunchroom and go back to my solo lunch by the window. But I don't like to judge people by first impressions. Unlike this girl. I'll be the better person. I'll stay. I'll at least *try* to make a new friend.

"Oh, I'm Krystal," she says. Not offering up her last name. Maybe she doesn't have one. Maybe she's just Krystal. It's probably with a K. "With a K." Yep.

"Do you have a pump?" I ask as I pull mine out again and type in my carbs for the lunch Mom packed.

"Duh," Krystal with a K says. "I've got a patch pump. The tubing was just too much for me, you know? Such a pain with dresses."

I nod as if I know what she's talking about. As if I've had my pump for more than two days.

And I wonder if I should have picked a patch pump. Maybe I should have let Cai make that pros and cons list after all.

"Um, are you even listening?" Krystal with a K asks.

"Yeah, totally." I wasn't. I'm not. This sucks. I thought it would be like being with other magic kids for the first time. I thought we'd be able to talk about things only we would understand. I thought I wouldn't have to explain. And instead I just feel judged and shamed.

I let Krystal with a K go on and on about her strict low-carb regimen and her workout routine. Apparently she has a bunch of followers on Instagram too. Her mom made her an account when she was diagnosed when she was seven. That seems kinda messed up to me, but she seems really into it. So I try not to judge. I fail. But I do try.

There's a moment when she's talking about the grain-free low-carb crackers her mom makes from scratch when I almost mention that my family got pizza to celebrate my pump. Just to see the look on her perfect face. But the more I think about it, the more I realize it would just be even more of an opportunity for her to judge me. She's already basically said I'm a bad diabetic.

"Well, I'm gonna go," Krystal with a K says. "See you around, Betty."

"It's Ber," I correct her. But she's not listening. She's grabbing her pink designer backpack and walking away. Perfect blond hair swinging as she goes. And as I watch her, my heart sinks. Krystal is the first diabetic I've ever met. At least the first type one. And I hate her. She's the worst. She's not some soulmate who can understand me like my other friends can't. She's kinda mean. And really boring.

And then I have a series of terrible, wonderful ideas.

I glance around the lunchroom. I'm alone. Almost everyone has already gotten up to go to class. The nearest group of kids is three tables away.

First, I put all the diet sodas in my bag. I prefer the sugar ones and just shooting the insulin for them. But I'm not turning down free soda.

Next, I take out my meter. The Sir Ber bag with the tiny lady knight is a bit dingy and faded; I should wash it. And I should change my lancet—the tiny bit of metal that stabs my hand. But I know I won't be doing either of those things anytime soon.

Then I pull out my phone and scroll through iDemon, the demon identification and reference app my cousins in Ireland made.

I don't have to scroll very far. Annoyances are in my "recent searches." And they're a class A. And I know I shouldn't. I know that with my brain. But my heart? My heart knows the truth. Krystal with a K deserves this.

> A little chaos to create
> Until the target is irate.
> Silly pranks and sneaky tricks
> Hilarious hijinks in the mix
> Confuse, confound, and cause some stress
> Until her hair's a total mess.

I prick my ring finger and watch the blood well, catching it with the waiting test strip. But once the strip has drunk its fill, the blood keeps coming. And coming. I shove my finger into my mouth, wondering if I have a Band-Aid in my bag somewhere. I haven't had a bleeder this bad in a hot second. But maybe there was a tiny bit of adrenaline driving me on as I stabbed my finger. Perhaps just an itty bitty bit of pettiness too. And I'm not sure if it was the extra blood or the less-than-ideal state of mind, but I've overshot my spell a bit.

The demon that swoops into the mortal dimension is not an Annoyance. For one, it has wings. And I've never seen an Annoyance with wings. I know it's a Mischief demon; the bright green eyes give it away. There are six of them, and they blink at me slowly, a chaotic gleam in each and every one. The Mischief demon also has a single, spiraling horn and a long, swishing tail. And it's as big as Clío. I'm suddenly glad she stayed home today. The demon is such a deep purple it's almost black. Its eyes move from mine and turn toward the doors of the lunchroom. Its wings unfurl. They're thin and nearly translucent, like a bat's. Once they're fully extended, they've got to be five feet wide. The demon takes one look back at me, flexes its shining silver claws, and then takes off.

Well, this is not great. It's not even good. It might actually be very, very bad.

I'm frozen. I don't know what to do. The obvious answer is to go after the demon and banish it. But maybe it'll be fine. Maybe it'll just tickle Krystal a bit and then go back to the demon dimension. No real harm done. Maybe I can just go to class and—

"Ber, what was that?" Cai's voice breaks through my shock. My relief at seeing him mixes with my anger that he hasn't texted me back. And then the guilt and fear about the demon I've just conjured bully all the other emotions away.

"Is it because I wasn't there?" Cai asks. "The accidental? I felt it. I was looking for you. I wanted to explain why I haven't—"

"It wasn't an accidental," I cut him off. His eyebrows disappear into his floppy black hair.

"You *meant* to conjure that demon?" he hisses.

"Well, I meant to conjure *a* demon," I whisper back. "But I might have let my emotions get the better of me and . . ." I trail off. Can I tell Cai what I've done? Won't he know anyway, even if I don't want to tell him?

He waits for me to explain.

"I conjured an Annoyance demon to annoy the other diabetic kid, Krystal. With a K."

"Oh!" Cai's face brightens. "Well, that's no big deal then. An Annoyance is easy to banish, right? We just have to go track it down and . . ." He trails off as I shake my head.

"Well, I meant to conjure an Annoyance," I explain. "But I'm pretty sure I just conjured a class D Mischief demon and sent it after Krystal."

"And what's a class D?"

"A Devilry."

CHAPTER EIGHT
a devilry of a banishing

"Should we call your mom?" Cai asks.

"Absolutely not." Mom is the very last person I want to know about what I've just done.

"Should we call my mom?"

"Obviously no." I roll my eyes. "There's no way she wouldn't tell mine. We just need to banish that Devilry."

"Well, yeah," Cai agrees. "But how?"

"Once we find it, it should be easy," I say. "Banishings are usually pretty simple." I'm walking toward the doors now and Cai hurries to come along. "I've never technically banished a Devilry before, but it shouldn't be much harder than an Annoyance."

"So we just need to find this Krystal person?" Cai asks.

"Assuming the Devilry understood its intended

target." I drop my voice; even if most of what I'm saying would sound like nonsense to geenin, it's best not to risk it.

"And why were you conjuring Mischief demons with intended targets in the first place?" Cai asks.

I glare at him as we make our way through the crowded hall.

"Fine, no explanations necessary," Cai says. I wonder if it's because he feels the residue of shame and anger still burning inside me from my lunch with Krystal. Or if he can hear my thoughts about him, which are less kind than I'd like them to be but feel pretty darn reasonable.

Unfortunately, I don't see Krystal or the Devilry anywhere.

"Do you know Krystal?" Cai starts asking random students as we walk through the hall.

He gets a lot of shaken heads and "Krystal who?" before someone finally nods and says, "Yeah, Krystal Christenson?"

"Krystal's last name is Christenson?" I ask.

"I mean, that's what we're trying to figure out, isn't it?"

"Blond? Impossibly perfect eyeliner? Designer backpack?" I contemplate adding a few more things, but this kid seems to be her friend, so I keep the other descriptions to myself.

They laugh. "Yep, that's Krystal. She even does

makeup tutorials on socials. You should check them out."

There is no dimension where I will be checking out Krystal with a K's makeup tutorials. But her friend doesn't need to know that.

"Super cool! Any idea what class she has next?" Cai asks.

"Yeah, we both have Language Arts. Why? Do you need me to tell her something?"

"I think she accidentally took my . . . phone," I invent wildly. Cai gives me a *really?* look that I totally ignore.

"Okay! Wanna walk with me?" Krystal's friend seems completely unfazed by my terrible lie, thank the goddess. We all walk down the hall, and Cai and Krystal's friend fall into easy conversation. That's something I love and hate about Cai. How easily he can just get along with anyone. Though maybe being able to magically sense how people are feeling and improve their mood could have something to do with that.

"Or maybe I'm just that charming," he whispers as we reach the Language Arts classroom. And I laugh before I remember that I'm mad at him for ghosting me for the last two days. But the laugh dies in my throat when Cai opens the door and I see Krystal cowering in the back of the classroom. It's obvious she can't see the demon, which is using its tail to knock random items in her direction, but she can definitely see the items flying through the air—seemingly under their own power.

"Um, Cai, a little help?" I murmur.

"On it," he says immediately. And I think he's going to do some mind mage something or other, but instead he does something even more effective. He starts to sing.

His voice isn't half bad. Actually, it's pretty darn good. He's singing something about dancing through life, which I assume is from some musical. He's weaving through the classroom, making his way to Krystal. And I take full advantage of his distraction.

As Cai reaches her, taking her hand and leading her away from the demon, the demon tries to follow, but I block its path, trying to meet all six of its lime-green eyes.

Cai's voice rises, belting out lyrics that are actually pretty clever. But I can't think about that right now. I need to focus. I think back through the conjuring I absolutely should not have done at all, never mind at school. I mentioned her hair being a mess.

Maybe if I can mess up her hair, the demon will think its purpose is fulfilled. But I'd have to get to Krystal first, and the Devilry is going to make that impossible.

The Devilry flaps its shiny wings, preparing for liftoff.

"Not so fast," I mutter. I gather saliva, imagining lemons, limes, and all other manner of citrus. And then I spit.

> You've been a bother and a blight,
> Begone thou Devilry from my sight.

The Devilry blinks all of its now very angry-looking eyes and calmly wipes the spit from its horn with an elegant foreleg.

Okay, well, that didn't work. I only know one other Mischief demon banishment by heart. I run through the words in my head as Cai's voice breaks on a high note and there's a smattering of applause.

I imagine the sourest lemon I've ever eaten and lunge, just as the demon darts to my left. My piddly little puddle of spit splatters the demon's wings as they nearly collide with my face.

> Purpose served, mischief achieved,
> From this dimension thou art cleaved.

I say the banishing as quickly and as quietly as I can, and there's a horrible moment where I think this one has failed too. The demon flies straight for Krystal, going in for a full-on tackle, but before it can reach her, it's pulled—tail first—back through the Veil, into the demon dimension.

I could cry from relief, but then Krystal's whiny voice breaks through my momentary happiness.

"Oh my god, did you spit on me? What is wrong with you?"

I have no idea what to say. I stand there, mouth hanging open. My brain is completely blank.

"Just a sneeze," Cai says quickly, stepping up beside me. "Isn't it so awkward when your girlfriend is allergic to your singing voice?" He starts to make the awkward turtle hand gesture, placing one hand on top of the other and wiggling his thumbs, but I slap his hand down.

"You two are dating?" Krystal's impeccable eyebrows come together, and she frowns as she looks between us.

"Yep." Cai grabs my slapping hand with his slapped one, interlacing our fingers. Proud to be holding my hand as the rest of the class starts to lose interest and the teacher arrives.

Krystal shrugs, and I bet her thoughts are saying *What is she doing with him?* Because I'm pretty sure that's what everyone's thinking when they see us. And I don't like that thought, and I don't even really believe it. But Cai is conventionally attractive, and no matter how many plus-sized influencers I add to my social media feeds, sometimes I just feel like we don't belong together.

Cai tugs my hand and leads me out of the classroom and into the hall just as tears start to prick my eyes.

"Don't think those things," Cai says. We're alone in the hall and I know that won't last for long. We need to get to class.

"Wait, think what things exactly?" I ask.

"Oh, ummm . . ." Cai's cheeks go super red as he trails off and runs a hand through his hair. "Well, it's just when your emotions get really strong, your thoughts get . . . really loud?" I start to reply but he cuts me off. "And really, really not true."

I start to pull my hand from his.

"No, seriously, Ber." He squeezes my hand tighter. "I know better than most that there are lots of people who think really mean things about other people who don't look or act like them. But you want to know something kinda wild? Something that makes it easier?"

I nod, not willing to trust my voice right now.

"They're almost always thinking way worse things about themselves."

"Really?"

He nods.

"I'm sorry *she* was the diabetic kids' lunch," he adds. "She seems . . ."

"Terrible? Mean?"

"Like someone I don't really want to hang out with," Cai says. Which is possibly the meanest thing I've ever heard him say about anyone.

"Are you going to tell me why you've been ghosting me?" I ask.

And then Cai's face does something weird. It takes me a second to register the emotion there because it's so out of character for him. He's sad. Like, really, *really* sad. Oh no, is he breaking up with me?

"No," he says quickly. "I'm not breaking up with you. Sorry, I said I would try to stay out of your head." He shakes his own head and bites his lip. "I'll tell you tomorrow, okay? My mom said you could come over. If you want."

"Okay," I say. My voice is small and strange and I fight to keep all my other selfish questions from pouring out of my mouth, or even pushing too hard into my mind. Cai's clearly upset, and I need to remember he has his own problems that aren't my missing grandma and Mystery demon.

"I'll text you, okay?" he says. Then he rushes down the hall, and I try to pretend it's because he's late for class and not because he's running away from me and all my messy, selfish problems.

CHAPTER NINE
being a really bad girlfriend

"Are you sure this is the address?" Maeve asks. It's Saturday morning and she's been "turned into a taxi," as she put it. Which really just means Mom and Dad asked her to drop me off at Cai's house. Maeve stares out the window of the car. We're stopped in front of a little triangle of land that sits at the southwest corner of the Slant Streets.

"Yeah, it's invisible until you've been invited, and even sometimes then," I say.

"But it's there?"

"Yep." I grab my bag and open the door. "Thanks for the ride. Say hi to Tempest for me." I open the back door and Clío hops out.

"Text if you need anything," Maeve says. "And

you're absolutely certain I'm not leaving my kid sister on a random street corner?" she adds, rolling down the window as I walk toward the house that only I can see.

Cai's house is on one of the Missoula thin places. Which are places where the Veil between dimensions is thinnest. The Slant Streets—a wonky neighborhood in Missoula where the streets go diagonal instead of straight across—are bordered by a thin place. Which just about anyone in Missoula could tell you, even if they aren't magical. The edges of the Slant Streets are *strange*. It's just that it's even stranger than most geenin realize.

And that's where Cai's house is. On a thin place. Or maybe it's *in* a thin place? I never fully follow the magical theory of all of it when he explains. It's especially confusing because mind mages only deal with magic of this dimension, so I'm not certain why they care about thin places in the first place. I just hope Maeve doesn't freak out too much as I step up onto the porch of the Andersons' big gray-green house, because I'm pretty sure it's going to look like I disappear.

I turn and see my sister's raised eyebrows. She can't see me anymore, but that seems to be all the proof she needs that she's safely delivered me to the right place. She smiles and waves at a spot a few feet to my right, and then drives away. Being a witch is weird.

I walk across the wide porch and have barely lifted my hand to knock when the dark blue door swings open.

"Ber, it's lovely to see you!" Greta stands in the doorway, opening her arms for a hug. Then she drops them and steps back, motioning me inside. "And you too, Clío."

I'm still not fully used to just how powerful Greta's magic is. I'd only internally flinched at the idea of a hug the teeniest, tiniest bit. And only for a second. But that was enough. I don't mind that I won't have to hug her though. Sometimes you just don't want to hug people. Or at least I don't. Even when they help you get an insulin pump with secret semilegal magic.

"Cai's in the living room," Greta says. "I made you guys some popcorn, but I left the box on the counter in case you need it for carb counts."

"Thanks so much," I say as she closes the door and starts toward the stairs.

"I'll be up in my office if you need me."

"We won't," Cai says brightly.

Greta laughs as she disappears upstairs and I smile as Cai takes my hand and leads me down the hall and into the living room. Even though I know where we're going. I was here last weekend. But I think he just likes holding my hand. Which is nice.

We settle onto the beige couch and Clío curls up

in the bed Greta got especially for her. Her ginger fur matches the neutral tones of the Andersons' extremely clean, extremely organized house. I swear Clío's even better behaved when we're over here. The house practically demands it. Though it could be due to Cai and his mom's ability to talk to her, or communicate with her—or whatever it is mind mages can do with animals. Which I'll always be insanely jealous of.

"How's she been with the pump stuff?" Cai asks.

"Fine," I say quickly, and then I launch into the speech I was practicing in my head all night last night, and all morning. And really every minute since Cai and I parted ways at school yesterday. "Okay, I know you have other things going on, and you really don't have to tell me everything about your life. We've only been . . . dating." I trip over the word a little bit but push on anyway. "I know we've only been dating for a little bit, and I never want you to feel like you have to tell me everything. But the last few days have been really intense and you were just gone, and didn't text me back. And then yesterday you said you were going to text me, and then you didn't. And it just—" I break off and take a deep breath. Part of me wonders if I should say this last bit at all, but in some ways it's the most important part and so I just keep going. "Well, it doesn't seem fair. That you can read my mind, basically.

And then you can have secrets. I don't want to keep secrets from you, not exactly. But I really trusted you. I do trust you, I think. And . . . well, yeah."

Not exactly the amazing, compelling, standing-ovation-worthy performance I'd imagined. And the ending was really bad. But I can tell I got my point across because Cai tucks one leg up under him and turns to face me fully on the couch.

"I'm sorry," he says. And then he looks up at the ceiling for a while and I try really hard not to think any particular thing too long or too loud or to let my emotions be too much.

"They're not," he says. "You're not. It's just—"

And this is it. I know it. He wants to like me, but it's too hard. I'm too complicated.

"Ber, please, will you just let me explain."

"Cai! I'm not even saying anything. I don't know how to not think things."

"It was the anniversary of my dad's death," he says. And that does it. That stops my thoughts. But not my emotions. Because I feel really, truly terrible.

"Oh, Cai, I'm so—" I start, but he shakes his head.

"It was just really bad timing, with my mom taking my phone away, and then the anniversary, and—I know I wasn't there for you. And I'm really sorry about that, but—"

"It's okay," I say. "Really."

"It's not that I don't care about your grandma, and Fin," he adds. "I do. Like, I really do. I think you might be right about the birds and the key and all that but—" He swallows and shoves his hands into the front pocket of his hoodie. "I just get really weird on October twentieth every year. And I wanted to mention it to you, but with you getting your pump and all the stuff that happened at the ritual . . . I dunno. I just didn't want you to think I was weird for getting as upset as I do. I mean, it was ten years ago, I don't even really remember him."

"Cai, no." I fight to keep my emotions as calm as I can; the last thing Cai needs right now is me bombarding him with even more feelings. "I'm sorry. I didn't know."

"I'm sorry I didn't tell you," he says. And then we sit there in silence for a while. And it feels like maybe things are going to be okay. At least with us. At least for now.

"Do you do something special?" I ask. "On the anniversary?"

"Yeah," he says, and there are tears in his eyes, but he also looks happy. "We go to the spot where my mom spread his ashes. And when we were there, this eagle landed on the tree and, Ber, his mind *felt* like Fin's. And I've been so excited to talk to you about it, but I've also just been sad and I didn't want to tell you over text."

"It's okay," I say, and I try really hard not to let a whole pile of questions pour out of my mouth. I just want to be a good, supportive girlfriend. But I've never been close to anyone my age who has lost a parent before.

"You are a good, supportive girlfriend," Cai says.

"Um, this is totally not the point right now, I know that. But . . . how much of my thoughts can you actually understand?"

Cai's quiet for a long time. A very long time. So long that I almost consider taking my question back. Not that that's possible. But I could change the subject or tell him I don't care no matter what. Did I just totally mess up my first boyfriend-girlfriend relationship? I'm about to wriggle out of my skin I'm so uncomfortable, which I know Cai can also probably sense.

"I'm trying not to." His voice is super quiet, so quiet he doesn't even sound like himself. "It's just . . . the closer I get to someone, the more open their mind gets, the more open your mind is getting. To me anyway. But sometimes . . . yeah."

"Yeah, what?" I ask.

"Sometimes I'm reading your mind. As in full phrases and thoughts, not just ideas or feelings."

"Oh," I say. And then I try something. *Can you hear this?* I think.

And then Cai nods. And I try to calm down, but all I

want to do is run away. Because I trust Cai, I really *really* like him. Heck, maybe I could even love him? And now my face is burning, because he can hear all of this, or some of it, but any of it is enough to make me want to shrivel up into a ball and throw myself into the ocean, even though the ocean is like a thousand miles away.

"We're actually less than five hundred miles from the ocean," Cai says.

"Cai!" I clamp my hands over my mouth when I realize I basically just screamed his name. We both look up, waiting for Greta's footsteps to come rushing down the stairs. But she doesn't seem to have noticed. "Is this normal?" I ask.

"I mean, is anything about being a magical teenager normal?" he asks. "But I know what you mean, and no. My mom thinks it has something to do with spending time with Fin, even though it was only a few days."

"Oh wow," I say. "So, it's not just, like, normal mind mage powers? Because your mom's seem pretty intense."

Cai laughs, and it's the best sound I've heard all day.

"Oh, yeah, my mom is powerful," he says. "But what's happening with me is . . . different."

"And it's my fault?" I ask. "Well, mine and Fin's?"

"I think fault is the wrong word," Cai says. "But I'm not sure what the right one is either."

"Yeah, I guess."

"But the birds," Cai says, and it's almost like he's his normal self again. Not that his sad self isn't his normal self. That's super not-fair. And if that's the case, I'm not my normal self either. Not without Grandma Orla. I shove the thoughts away as I try to keep up with what Cai's saying.

"It didn't make sense at first, because the owl—you know, the one that ran into the window? Well, it wasn't really thinking or picturing much of anything. I just kept hearing *who, who, who*. Which is just the sound an owl makes, right?"

"Yeah," I agree. "And I guess it had just hit its head pretty hard."

"Exactly." Cai's eyes widen as he keeps talking. "But then the eagle at my dad's tree; it kept thinking about books. And, like, why would an eagle even know about books? And it just sat there for a long time. And I hadn't seen your text yet, my mom hadn't given me back my phone. But then when I did, I started to wonder. Keys. Who. Books? The third line isn't about books though."

"'The key is the story you tell yourself,'" I recite. "'About who you are and who you may become.'"

"See? Two 'whos'!" Cai says. "And wouldn't it be just *so* Fin to play with language, even when they're trying to relay a message or clues or whatever."

"Yeah, maybe," I say. And then I make the connection. "Stories! Books hold stories. The third line is 'Lives are stories.'"

"Yes!" Cai agrees. And it feels like we're really onto something. But as we keep puzzling through it, we start to lose steam. Because the clues are just reminding us of Fin's Prophecy. Which we already have.

"They're pointing to particular words in the lines though," Cai says. "Maybe we should go somewhere with lots of birds?" He frowns, but then brightens. "Or! Or, or, or! We should ask Phoebe. The next line starts with 'rooted.'" He gains speed as he recites the next three lines. "'Rooted in the telling, but also changed.'" He ticks off the line on his hand. "'Clutched too tightly, stories cannot *grow*,'" he continues, with lots of emphasis on the last word. "'And *grow* they must,'" he finishes. "Yeah, you definitely should come hang with me and Phoebe tomorrow. At her house. She'll help us crack this case wide open."

Hearing Cai already had plans with Phoebe tomorrow twists something in my gut that feels an awful lot like jealousy. Even though they were friends first. Even though they're only friends. So I try not to feel jealous, but trying not to feel things is really hard. Maybe completely impossible. And I can see the moment Cai feels what I'm feeling.

"No, that sounds great," I say. "I'll be there. It's a great idea." My voice is too happy, and I know he can sense what I'm feeling, but he doesn't say anything. And I wish I could read his mind. And even though I know it's totally selfish, I'm still kind of sad and angry. But Cai doesn't take those complicated emotions away, even though I'm sure he can feel them. And that just makes me even more confused.

CHAPTER TEN

good, bad, and complicated

"Isn't cereal one of the worst possible things for your blood sugar?" Maeve asks.

"Yep." I shovel another big bite of cereal into my mouth. "But I have my pump now," I say through the crunchy mush. Once I swallow, I add, "And sometimes what is bad for my blood sugar is absolutely necessary for my mental health. And my spirit. And, you know, my will to live."

"Okay, okay, I get it." Maeve laughs and pours herself a bowl.

"But yeah, I'll probably regret this," I say through another mouthful. "Even with my pump."

"Eh, sometimes things are just worth it," Maeve says.

I nod and we eat our cereal in silence for a while.

Well, not quite silence; there's lots of chomping, but no talking. Which gives me the opportunity to think. Which doesn't always feel like a good thing lately.

"How are things with Tempest?" I ask.

Maeve's eyebrows scrunch together, suspicion clear on her face.

"I just mean, being out to our families, and not having the same magic . . ."

"Did something happen with Cai?" Maeve asks. Sometimes Maeve's sisterly instincts are a bit too on point.

"I mean, no," I say into my cereal bowl. Suddenly the slightly soggy flakes are looking less appealing. "Not really."

"Not really but kind of yes?" Maeve asks.

"No, not kind of yes," I say.

"But not no?" Maeve asks. And she's almost as infuriating as Fin sometimes. So infuriating that I almost blurt out the truth. But then I stop. I don't know if I should tell Maeve the extent of Cai's powers. I'm not sure I should tell anyone. It's not like it's his fault. Just like my accidental demons aren't my fault. But I still wish I could talk with her about it. Maybe I still can.

"I'm just struggling with his magic," I finally say. "The way he can always sense how I'm feeling and stuff. It's hard when you can't keep anything from someone. Not that I want to keep things from him . . ."

Maeve lets out a *hmm* sound and nods. "Oh, okay, yeah, that tracks. And it sounds super complicated. And honestly, things with Tempest and me are . . . tricky."

"Wait, really?" I can't decide if I'm relieved to hear Maeve's also struggling, or sad that things with Tempest aren't as perfect as they appear from the outside. I don't want my sister to feel bad, but even just with that one phrase, I feel less alone.

"We got into a fight last night." Maeve stirs her cereal around her bowl. I force myself to take a few more bites while I wait for her to be ready to say more. I shot enough insulin for the whole bowl, so I have to at least try to finish it.

"I didn't realize that she actually believes a bunch of the stuff her moms do about blood witches," Maeve says. "I was telling her about Cai crashing our Blood Moon gathering and it just got . . . weird? It's hard to explain." She chomps on more cereal before she drops her spoon into her bowl. "I know she doesn't want to believe those things, and I know she loves me. And I think we can get through it. But I can't figure out if she just . . . I dunno. Thinks I'm a bad person for practicing blood magic."

"Wait, seriously?"

"I'm not sure how much you know about weather

magic," Maeve says, pushing her bowl aside entirely. I'm jealous. I'd give just about anything not to finish this soggy cereal.

"I know some of what Grandma Orla thinks about weather witches," I say before I take another mushy bite.

"Yeah, so, Grandma Orla had—has," she corrects quickly when I glare at her. "Grandma Orla has her prejudices, but weather witches . . ." She trails off and then throws up her hands. "Well, they're hypocrites. Grandma Orla was right about that."

"Because they won't conjure demons?" I ask. Whenever Grandma Orla talks about weather witches she's always talking about how they just need to own their power and conjure properly, as if pulling weather between dimensions isn't real magic.

"Because they claim that conjuring demons is unethical, that we don't understand the implications of pulling beings between dimensions—but they don't know how blood magic even works. Which, fair, Tempest has a point that that is partly because we're so freaking secretive about all of it—but still!" Maeve throws her hands up again and nearly knocks Frangi off the counter where she's been eyeing the milk left at the bottom of my bowl. "So we got in a big fight about it. And we both said some things we probably regret. But I just don't think you can claim pulling demons through the Veil is bad when you pull entire weather systems from multiple dimensions." She turns to me. "Did you know that? That the weather they pull doesn't just come from one particular dimension? Like, they could be causing floods or droughts or, I don't know, but it could be just as bad as what we do. Not that what we do is bad," she adds quickly.

"I think good and bad are a lot more complicated than I realized," I say.

"Seriously," Maeve agrees. She traces little circles on the countertop with her finger and we sit in silence for a bit. "I'm sorry about you and Cai though," she says. "I really hope you can figure it out. I like him."

"Yeah," I agree. "So do I. Which is kinda part of the problem."

I look up at Maeve and she's biting her lip. I can tell there's something else she wants to say. When she doesn't volunteer the information, I finally ask. "What else aren't you saying?"

"You're going to hate me if I tell you," she says.

My stomach clenches. I could never hate Maeve, but now I have to know even more.

"Well, now you have to tell me, 'cuz whatever I'm imagining is probably worse than whatever you could say."

There's a long pause before Maeve sighs and finally says, "It's easier dating Tempest with Grandma Orla not here."

Okay, maybe I was wrong. Maybe what Maeve actually had to say was worse than anything I could have imagined.

"I knew it," I say. "You're all glad she's gone. You promise me you'll help get her back, but then you actually don't even want to." I'm so mad my hands are shaking. I was planning on inviting her to Phoebe's house. I wanted to get her amazing brain back in on the puzzle of Fin's Prophecy. But she's actually not even interested at all.

"No! Ber! That's not true. And see? I knew you'd be mad. This is why I don't talk about it with you. You think any criticism of Grandma Orla means we don't want her back."

"I know Grandma Orla isn't perfect," I snap. "And I know Fin is complicated. I'm not saying either of them are perfect."

"I'm not saying you are!"

We both start talking at the same time. And stop. And start again.

"I just feel like I'm the only one who cares about really getting her back," I say once Maeve waves a hand for me to talk.

"You aren't," Maeve insists. "Mom misses her more than you give her credit for, she just doesn't want to admit it to us. You know her. She's always gotta be strong and whatever."

I try to interrupt but Maeve keeps talking.

"I'm not saying that we don't miss her. I miss her. I want her back. But I also can't lie and say it isn't easier dating a weather witch without Grandma Orla here to glare at her, or at me. And I'm not dishonoring her or anything by saying that."

And I wonder if I should tell her about the clues. Tell her about Cai and the birds and why I'm going to Phoebe's later today. But before I can make up my mind, Clío comes running into the kitchen, Mars hot on her heels. They just barely miss crashing into the counter and Mars leaps up. I'm about to hold out a hand to each of them for equal opportunity to alert when my pump lets out a shockingly loud series of beeps. I pull it off the waistband of my pants and see two arrows pointing straight up. Guess not even the extended bolus feature was a match for cereal. Oh well. I don't regret it. Cereal is awesome.

Since I need to test to verify what my sensor and dog and cat are all telling me, Maeve and I use the drop of blood to conjure a Tidy. It takes ages for my blood sugar to come back down, but I don't actually have to do anything. My sensor was right, and my pump takes care of all of it. It's basically magic. And even though the pump is a bit awkward, and I've gotten the tubing caught on at least three door handles already this morning, I love having an insulin pump.

PART TWO

The Pain of Knowing Just a Little

CHAPTER ELEVEN

up the rattlesnake

I take it back. I hate having a pump. Mom offered to help me with the refill, but I have to figure out how to do it on my own. There are just too many dang steps.

"Don't forget to *thwap* the syringe to get the bubbles out," Mom says.

"I wasn't going to forget," I grumble. It's a lie. I was totally right in the middle of skipping that step. Even though it's written on the step-by-step instructions sitting next to me. But at least half the paper and plastic I've ripped from all the different fiddly little parts of the cartridge are scattered over the table.

"Sure is a lot of detritus involved in this whole insulin pump thing," Dad says.

"De-what-is?" I've finally got the newly filled cartridge into the pump.

"Detritus," Dad repeats. "It means . . . well, lots of stuff. But discarded stuff. Not quite trash, but sometimes trash?"

Sounds like a Fin word. The thought flashes through my mind before I can stop it. I'm trying not to think about Fin. Or Grandma Orla. And fail. I wonder if I should tell my parents the real reason I'm going to Phoebe's house today. But I immediately decide against it. I have to bring them real evidence. A real plan. Which we're going to find today.

As if summoned by my thoughts, my phone buzzes on the table with a text from Cai. He's probably asking where I am. I was supposed to meet him and Phoebe at Phoebe's house half an hour ago. There's a tiny part of me that wants to cancel. Cai sent me a video from some diabetes YouTuber who calls it "playing the diabetes card." She also says if we have to live with diabetes, we might as well get some perks. Not that deciding not to hang out with your friends because you're so mentally exhausted you feel like you might cry is a perk. But most folks kind of shut up if you can't do something and just give some vague (or not so vague) diabetes reason. And the ones who don't are jerks anyway.

But my friends aren't jerks. They're my friends. And they care about me. And I do want to hang out with them. Mostly. I do definitely want to find out if Phoebe can help crack the code to Fin's Prophecy. She was a huge help saving my family from the Kalispell Coven last month, and her plant magic is really cool.

"Are you still up for going to Phoebe's?" Mom asks. The repeated beeps that go along with filling the tubing up with insulin finally stop as I see drops appear. Time to reconnect.

"Yeah, I still want to go." I clip the pump back into the site on my stomach. "I can still go, right?"

"Yep! Just make sure you have enough low snacks packed."

"Got 'em!" I hold up my backpack and Clío sits beside me, tail wagging.

"How far up the Rattlesnake do they live exactly?" Mom asks as we walk to the garage. The Rattlesnake is one of the coolest neighborhoods in Missoula, and it makes total sense that plant mages live up there.

"I'm not sure. I've never been to Phoebe's before. But my maps app says it'll take almost twenty minutes to get there. So pretty far?" For a moment I'm worried Mom might change her mind, but she just sighs and climbs into the car, and we're off to drop me at my plant mage friend's house. A lot can change in a few weeks.

"I'll be back at four thirty," Mom says as Clío and I stand on the curb beside Phoebe's house. Which is huge and looks like something out of a movie. A towering thorny hedge blocks most of the house from view, but it's at least four stories, with whimsical turrets and plants of all kinds growing on and around it. It's deep purple with mint-green accents.

"Thanks, Mom," I say, and I try to make it clear I'm saying thanks for more than just driving me, but I'm not sure if she can tell or not. She smiles and waves and I turn and walk through the arching gap in the deep green hedge.

The yard on the other side of the hedge is incredible. There is no doubt that plant mages live here. There's no other way to explain the riot of colors and shapes. And the fact that there are plants from every climate I can imagine. I'm absolutely certain palm trees don't grow in Missoula. And there shouldn't be this many things blooming in late October. They must have magical help.

As I walk up the front path, I hear my name.

"Ber, Ber, up here!" Cai is whisper-yelling to me from a window on the second story of the house. "This way, over here!"

"What? Why?" I ask as I cross through the yard. Careful not to step on any of the flowers. Which there are a lot of. Phoebe's head appears beside Cai's and they both shush me.

"Wait, am I sneaking in?" I hiss up at them. "I thought I was invited!"

"You are," Phoebe whisper-shouts. "But my grandma didn't realize you're a blood witch and then there was this whole thing and just . . . it's fine, you'll just need to climb up."

She points at a trellis that runs up the side of the purple house. Up to the window where my friends are smiling and waving as if climbing up a rickety old trellis is a totally normal way to enter your friend's house. A bit of roof sticks out, making a tiny platform outside the window.

They want me to climb up the trellis, scuttle across the roof, and climb in the window?

"Um, hello?" I shake my head and point to Clío.

"The vines will get her," Phoebe says. "Come on, quick. Just put your hands—or paws for her—on the base of the trellis and let the wisteria help!"

Cool. Sure. Just let the magical plants lift me and my dog fifteen feet into the air. This is not what I signed up for when I agreed to hang out at Phoebe's house. I shake my head, but then look up at my friends' smiling faces.

"It's fun!" Cai insists. "And I just told Clío what's gonna happen. She's ready!"

"Well, that makes one of us," I mutter. But I step over an amethyst-purple flower and place my hands on the trellis. The vines twine around my wrists and lift. I don't know whether to grab on to anything or not but decide to just let the plants do their thing. To my left, Clío's eyes are wide, and she snips experimentally at one of the plants but seems pretty unbothered.

"Really?" I ask her as we rise. "You're fine with this, but Movement demons freak you out? We have to work on that."

The vines deposit us onto the little patch of roof and Phoebe hauls my dog in through the window. Then Cai reaches out a hand to pull me through, right when I feel a horrible tug.

I curse and drop Cai's hand, reaching for my stomach. There's a sharp, awful pain, and when I look down, I see my insulin pump tangled in the vines. Which are now retreating back down onto the trellis. The tubing dangles uselessly, ripped from my skin.

"Phoebe, come quick, the vines have Ber's pump!" Cai calls into the room beyond the window.

"Oh no." Phoebe reappears and climbs out the window, joining me on the tiny patch of roof that is absolutely not big enough for both of us. She seems utterly unbothered by this fact and scooches by me, inches from the edge and a horrible drop.

"Give that back," she whispers, her voice stern. "Now!" she adds. After a moment she turns back to me, a wide smile on her round face. "Here you go!" She hands me the pump as if it's no big deal. And I don't even know what to say. I can't even tell what I'm feeling. I just need to get off this roof.

"Take this," I say, shoving the pump into Cai's hands. "And get out of the way."

He takes the pump and scrambles back from the window. I climb over the ledge. My backpack gets stuck on the window for a moment, but Phoebe pushes it down and gives me a little shove and then I'm in.

The room is as full of plants as the yard outside. There are two canopy beds. The one to the left is covered in dark green vines with small purple flowers that perfectly match the purple velvet bedspread. The bed to the right is covered in yellow-green leaves and huge white blooms.

Phoebe climbs in after me and crosses to that bed, plopping down onto the fluffy white quilt.

"You really don't want to eat that," Phoebe says to Clío, who's sniffing a plant by the window. "Or even smell it."

"Then what's it doing in your room?" I ask, pulling my dog away. "Isn't it a bit weird to have a poisonous plant growing in your bedroom?"

"I know not to eat it or smell it," Phoebe says.

"She's a dog!" I practically shout. I drop my voice. "You should have warned me. I wouldn't have brought her."

"She'll be fine," Phoebe says with a shrug. "Cai can warn her about all the plants she should avoid, he's been over here enough times. And we don't have to be quiet anymore." She gestures toward the door, which is completely covered in thick moss. It seems to be moving, and I realize it is growing in to cover all the cracks around the door. "It blocks almost all sound, and Grandma should still be taking her nap."

"Good," I snap. "Because this was all not okay."

"Wait, what?" Cai looks up from where he's seated on the floor, probably explaining to Clío what plants could kill her if she took a totally normal exploratory nibble.

"Not warning me about having to get lifted up here by vines," I say. "My pump ripping out! Clío almost eating some plant that could kill her."

"We got your pump back," Phoebe says, crossing her arms. "And just because blood witches are ignorant of basic plant properties—"

"Watch who you're calling ignorant," I snap. "Do you have any idea what would have happened if my pump had fallen from that high? What I have to do now to put it back on?"

"Um, you just . . . clip it back on, right?" Phoebe's confident mask falters a bit, and she glances between me and Cai.

"It ripped out!" I shout. I lift up my fuzzy jacket and shirt and show her the spot on my stomach where the pump was attached. It's now just a red welt and a little tiny speck of a hole where the cannula went in. "I have to put in a whole new site. Thankfully I have one in my bag, or there'd be no way for me to get my insulin."

"Sorry," Phoebe mumbles. "I didn't realize."

"No, you didn't."

We're all quiet for a long moment as I open my backpack and find a new site.

"Can we help at all?" Cai asks.

"You can let me leave through the front door," I say, peeling off the layers of plastic and trying to decide where to stab the site. I don't want to put it too close to the place where the one just ripped out. It hurt. The adhesive that keeps the little plastic cannula in place is strong. But not as strong as magical people-and-dog-lifting vines, apparently.

"You could help focus my mind," I add. "In case it bleeds. The diabetes educator person said they shouldn't normally, but I am stabbing myself, so no guarantees."

"I can do that," Cai says quickly. "Whatever you need."

"I need my friends to understand how serious diabetes is," I snap. "And don't you dare take any of my anger while you're in my mind, Cai." I glare at him.

"Fair."

"And we understand how serious diabetes is." Phoebe's voice is soft, almost apologetic. But there's a hint of defensiveness in there too and it sets me off all over again.

"You seriously don't."

"My grandma actually has diabetes, and—" Phoebe starts, and I practically scream.

"Type two! It's not the same. It still sucks, and I wish your grandma didn't have to deal with that, but it's not the same."

"Yeah, it's really not," Cai says. "Like, there are some similarities, both have to do with insulin, but insulin resistance and your body not producing any insulin are super different. I could send you some YouTube videos about it."

"I'm just saying that I get it," Phoebe says.

"But you don't." I glare at her.

"You don't know what I do and don't—"

"I could die," I say. And it's not a shout. I wish it were. I wish I sounded strong and defensive and brave when I say it. But I don't. I sound scared. And I am.

"I mean, we all almost died in September," Phoebe says. "Blood witches aren't the only ones who take risks—"

"I'm not talking about risks," I say, cutting her off. "I'm talking about just being a diabetic. Surviving diabetes. If I give myself too much insulin. If I don't have insulin. Diabetics die. From diabetes. If I didn't have insulin I'd last a few days, a week, tops. If I give myself too much insulin, I could die in hours."

"Oh." Phoebe's voice is so quiet I almost don't hear it.

"Yeah. Oh." I turn to Cai. "Ready?" He nods.

I select a bit of skin on the side of my stomach, place the round piece of plastic over it, and squeeze the sides. Nothing happens. I squeeze again. Still nothing. On the third squeeze, the spring-loaded needle shoots into my skin and it hurts. The pain disappears almost immediately and Cai winces.

"You didn't have to do that," I say as I pull out the needle, smoothing the sticky patch into place.

"Least I could do," he says. "But I left your anger and whatnot. It's super reasonable that you're mad at us right now."

"Yeah, it is," Phoebe adds quickly. "I'm really sorry, Ber. I didn't understand. I don't understand. But I'll try."

I almost thank her, but I don't. I'm still too mad. And I know Cai can tell. But he doesn't say anything. I prime the little plastic bit with a drop of insulin and try to let my breathing return to normal.

"So . . . Phoebe and I were talking through some of the lines of Fin's Prophecy before you got here," Cai says. I can tell he's testing the waters, seeing if I'm ready to move on. And I am, but I'm also not. But I figure I can be both angry and curious at the same time. So I let Cai and Phoebe dive in as I make sure my insulin pump is fully connected.

CHAPTER TWELVE
when is a clue not a clue?

"Okay, so there's a lot of plant imagery in here." Cai settles onto the ground, pointing at a piece of paper where he's written out Fin's Prophecy. Phoebe and I join him on the floor and Clío walks over and lies down with her head resting on my knee. Which is probably one of the absolute best things about having a dog.

"Yeah, 'rooted in the telling' and 'stories cannot grow' and 'grow they must'?" Phoebe points to the fourth, fifth, and sixth lines. "That's a lot of plant metaphors for a Mystery demon."

"Hmm." I pull the paper closer to me, even though I have the whole thing memorized. "But we still don't know that much about Mystery demons," I say. "What if the demon dimension is full of plants?"

"That would be so cool," Phoebe says, her eyes bright.

"Okay, so if the birds are really giving me clues—" Cai starts.

"Which is low-key creepy," Phoebe mutters.

"And high-key awesome," Cai replies. "So far, we have 'key,' 'who,' and 'stories.' I stood outside in the back garden for a while when I first got here, hoping some more birds might find me, but it was just a bunch of house finches getting the out-of-season berries off the bushes."

"But are the clues telling us anything that isn't already in the prophecy?" I ask. "Or is it just Fin reminding us? I'm not sure they have the best handle on how time passes in our dimension. They kept saying things about being confused my grandma was already a grandma."

"Yeah," Cai agrees. "I actually got the sense that Fin doesn't really understand time at all. Like, they didn't let me into their mind much, but when they did, it was wild. Usually, human minds feel like they're pointed both forward and back, some more in one direction than the other. And animal minds are almost totally pointed forward. But minds always have a relationship to time, a feeling of our place in it, you know?"

"Not really," Phoebe says. "But I'm used to you taking at least five detours on your way to a point."

"Rude," Cai says, pretending to scowl. "But fair," he adds with a smile. "And I'm getting to a point, or really, a question. What if the clues aren't clues at all? What if they're just reminders?"

"It's only been a few weeks," I say. "It's not like we've forgotten about them." But then I pause, because isn't that exactly how it felt the other night when I came back from absolutely not snooping in Grandma Orla's house and the rest of my family was just happily making dinner? And isn't that how it felt when Maeve told me she's basically *relieved* Grandma Orla is gone?

"I just think we need to try to understand the nature of the clues before we start to try to decipher them, you know?" Cai looks between us, and I nod. He's probably right. But I can't help feeling a bit disappointed. I'd thought maybe we would put our heads together and figure it all out this afternoon. But I guess that was too much to hope for. I feel like I'm doing that a lot lately, hoping for too much. Everything is always too good to be true.

"I think you should start having some mugwort tea before bed," Phoebe says.

Cai and I both look at her, and then at each other. I'm glad I'm not the only one who doesn't understand. Phoebe does this though, just says something about plant magic as if we'll both understand it. She rolls her eyes before she explains and the flame of anger in my chest that I thought had burned out threatens to roar back to life.

"Remember when I first met you and Fin in September?" Phoebe asks.

We nod. How could I forget? Cai and Phoebe crashed movie day. And it was a good thing they did, because a few hours later a Diatribe arrived from Grandma Orla and my parents telling us they'd been taken hostage by the Kalispell Coven. And Cai and Phoebe were absolutely essential to getting them back and sort of, mostly defeating Lindley and her coven. If you can count letting them disappear into the demon dimension after my grandma "defeating." Which I'm not sure you can.

"Okay, so remember how Fin couldn't stay hidden from me?" Phoebe asks. I hadn't remembered that, but now that I do, I think I see what she's getting at.

"Because you'd had mugwort tea," I say. "Right? Isn't that what Fin said? Something about invisibility spells being powerless against mugwort?"

"Exactly," Phoebe says. "So, Cai, I think you should start drinking mugwort tea. It's a powerful plant, so make sure not to take too much at first."

"Do you have some?" Cai asks. "We don't do much with teas and tinctures and my mom's totally a coffee person."

"Duh," Phoebe says. "I'll send you home with some."

"Cool," Cai says. "I'll start drinking the tea and report back if there are any changes in the messages."

"Okay, but also . . ." Phoebe trails off and leans forward. Her voice is low, and she looks almost scared to say whatever she's going to say next. And I guess I did just freak out on her, but she did deserve it. My heart starts to race as Cai gestures for her to keep talking.

"I just can't help but wonder," Phoebe continues, "if they are messages, from the birds, you know? What if . . . well, what if it isn't Fin at all?"

"What do you mean?" Cai asks.

"What if it's someone or *something* else? Like, pretending to be Fin."

"Nah," Cai says, waving a hand. "That feels like too much of a coincidence. And I know what Fin's mind feels like, and that eagle *felt* like Fin. You wouldn't get it unless you were a mind mage."

"Maybe," Phoebe says. "But keys could mean a lot of things. What if the owl was just an owl? What if eagles are always thinking about books?"

"Okay, I don't get too many opportunities to feel an eagle's mind," Cai says. "I can't say for certain. But I'm pretty confident that they aren't thinking about books unless they're serving as messengers from our demon friend."

Phoebe and Cai keep arguing, and I want to interrupt, or contribute, or just . . . say *something*. It's my Mystery demon, my grandma, my family and magic. But I feel really weird. It takes a minute before I notice that Clío's been whining and pawing at my leg while Phoebe and Cai continue to bicker about what Fin's mind feels like.

I hold out a hand to my dog. Her nose bumps my palm. I look at my pump, wondering why it didn't alert me for the low. But I see an error on the screen. My sensor isn't working.

"Um, my sensor isn't working," I say as Clío grabs my pack.

"Oh, umm," Phoebe says, breaking off her argument with Cai and looking super guilty.

"Umm, what?" I ask as I grab a juice box out of my pack. I don't feel like eating. Liquid carbs it is. Even if juice boxes make me feel like a baby.

"I probably should have mentioned, but I didn't really realize . . ." She trails off, and if I weren't chugging my juice through its dinky little plastic straw, I'd throw the entire juice box at her. Yep, the anger flame is definitely back, and now it's practically a bonfire.

"Technology is super unreliable at our house," she says.

"Wait, like all technology?" I splutter, juice dribbling

down my chin. Scratch that, not a bonfire, a whole forest fire.

"Anything with a battery, or like Bluetooth, or radios, radios get super weird."

"My pump and sensor use Bluetooth and radio waves!"

"Sorry." Phoebe winces.

Cai looks between us, clearly worried we're about to start shouting at each other again, and I just might. Instead, I think some really awful things about Phoebe really loudly, hoping Cai can hear every word as I push myself off the floor, pull my jacket back on, and grab my pack.

"How do I get out of this house that isn't out the dang window?" I demand. "Since we can't even decide if the clues are clues and your house is basically trying to kill me, I want to go home and I'm *not* climbing out the window."

I can tell Phoebe is about to argue, but Cai gives her a look and she sighs and climbs off her bed.

The moss that had smothered the door retreats and she opens it tentatively, peeking her head out and looking back and forth.

"This way," she whispers.

I stomp toward the door. I don't care if her family hears me. I don't care if they hate me. I'm never coming back here ever again. And I'm totally not impressed by all the different types of plants filling every possible window, snaking along the ceiling, and wrapped around the beautiful, carved wooden banister as we walk down the stairs.

I'm completely indifferent to the cat that boops Clío's nose as we enter an extremely cozy living room filled with jewel-toned furniture and amazing paintings. I don't even pet the cat. I do. I pet the cat. Cai whispers that her name is Pawthos. And I absolutely do not giggle on the inside about it as I remain indifferent to her fluffy black-and-orange face.

"Ah, this must be Bernadette," a short woman with Phoebe's same sharp eyebrows and wide nose says. Obviously Phoebe's mom.

Phoebe makes a little squeak.

"Grandma, this is Ber," she says quickly. Okay, not her mom. Dang, our grandmas are either not the same age or I just am bad at guessing people's ages. "Ber, this is my grandma, Mai."

"Hi," I say. "I'm actually just leaving."

"I didn't hear you arrive," she says, looking pointedly at her granddaughter. Yep. That's my cue.

"I'll let Phoebe explain," I say quickly. "It was really nice to meet you." I give Pawthos one last scritch and then practically run out the front door, down the path, and out onto the street.

My hands are shaking when I text Mom, begging her to pick me up a couple of hours early. I know I'll have to sit out here in the cold for at least half an hour unless she happens to be somewhere close by, which is unlikely. But I don't even care.

She texts back that she's on her way almost immediately, like she was just waiting for me to text. Like she expected something like this to happen. And maybe she did. Maybe there's a reason blood witches don't hang out with plant mages. Maybe Grandma Orla was right. Maybe it would be better if I didn't hang out with Cai and Phoebe for a while. Not that I have any real geenin friends to replace them with. Not that I want to replace them. And maybe I need them, to get Grandma Orla back. But it's not like they were any real help today. And they actually made diabetes harder. Which I don't think friends are supposed to do.

Tears sting my eyes as I blink down at my phone and then my pump. My sensor is working again now that I'm not in the house.

I pace back and forth on the sidewalk down the street from the Fangs' house, and I keep glancing back up the street, expecting Cai to come check on me. But he doesn't. Maybe he's helping Phoebe explain. Maybe he's playing referee, using his mind mage powers to smooth things over. But whatever he's doing, he's not here. He's choosing Phoebe. And sure, they've been friends for years, they've known each other since they were kids.

But so have you, a stubborn part of my brain reminds me. Just because I only found out Cai was magic when Fin came to school with me last month doesn't mean I haven't known him since fifth grade. And he's supposed to be my boyfriend. He's supposed to be out here with me, making sure I'm okay.

I blink back tears as Mom pulls up, scratching Clío's ears.

"All okay?" Mom asks as we climb in.

"No." I shake my head, and my voice breaks on the single word. Mom takes the hint, squeezes one of my hands, and then puts on some music and drives me home.

CHAPTER THIRTEEN
keeping secrets

Cai texts me at least ten times that night. I ignore him. Which is hard. But then I decide to just turn off my phone completely and it gets a bit easier. My sensor talks to my pump too, so I still have my blood sugar. Besides, I want his texts to be breakthroughs, a surefire path to get Grandma Orla and Fin back. But I just know it will be excuses. And I'm not ready for that. So I shove my phone under my pillow and curl up with Mars and Clío and one of my favorite fantasy novels, *Strange the Dreamer*. There's a character in it who can enter people's dreams, and I wish I could do that. I wish I could find Grandma Orla in her dreams and tell her I haven't forgotten about her.

I fall asleep reading and when I wake up the next

morning, the book is tucked under my pillow, next to my phone. I decide I'm going to wait to turn it on. I did find Grandma Orla in my dreams, but not the way I was hoping for. All night I just had nightmare after nightmare of the Cataclysm demon that became the Tairseach—the rip between dimensions. I watched all of its sucking and chomping mouths reach for Grandma Orla, and unlike in September when she and Fin did big, terrifying magic and created the Tairseach, in my nightmares the Cataclysm reached all of its mouths out and gobbled my entire family, saving me for last.

It wasn't exactly a restful night.

I let Clío downstairs so she can go do her business in the yard as I take a shower and get ready for school. The place where my pump ripped out yesterday is still raw and stings a bit under the hot, soapy water. Halfway through my shower, my pump starts buzzing on the counter where I left it. By the time I rinse the conditioner out of my hair and towel off, it's practically buzzed its way right off the counter and onto the floor. I get to it just in time, expecting it to tell me my blood sugar is high.

Instead, there's an alert I haven't seen before.

Pump battery low.

Right. I have to charge it. Which means plugging it in for a while. I either have to sit attached to the plug, or leave my pump while it charges. I wish I'd thought of that before I showered. Now I'm not sure I'll have time to charge it before school.

I hurry through the rest of my morning routine and hope it isn't too cold outside since I absolutely don't have time to dry my hair all the way. I'm pulling my sweater over my head while walking down the stairs (and trying not to die) when I hear Mom's and Dad's hushed voices. I freeze, sweater still bunched around my shoulders.

"I'm really worried about her," Mom says. It's immediately clear from her tone that she's talking about me. That's her *Ber and diabetes* voice. "I think she's getting fixated on my mother and that Mystery demon."

I feel like I'm freezing and on fire at the same time. I'm definitely not supposed to be hearing this.

"You know how she is about Orla," Dad says.

"That's my point." Mom sets something down on the counter and her voice gets harder to hear. I take another two steps down the stairs, trying to stay out of sight but get a bit closer. But I miss whatever she says next.

"Maybe we should just tell her," Dad says. And my heart is pounding so hard I feel like I'm going to burst. Tell me what?

See? I want to shout. *They were hiding something.* I wish I could text Cai and tell him he was wrong, but my phone is still upstairs, and my parents are still talking, their voices even lower.

"I'm just worried this is all distracting her too much,"

Mom says. "Diabetes is complicated, more complicated than any of us realized. We need her to focus on that."

"But what happens when she finds out it's not a spell?" Dad says. "What happens when she finds out there isn't a way to solve the riddle? That this is exactly why Mysteries were banned from this dimension in the first place?"

Banned? What is he talking about?

"I've been through my mother's books at least a dozen times after the girls have gone to bed the last few weeks," Mom says. "I know we can't trust Mysteries, and I know Ber got attached to that demon. Can we really blame her?" She sighs, and I can't tell if I want to cry or scream or dissolve into a pile of sand. "I just don't want to kill Ber's hope when it's the only thing keeping her going. I know she really likes Cai, but Greta and I aren't sure what's going on between them. Ber wouldn't say what happened at Phoebe's, but I know it wasn't good."

"But isn't that why we should just tell her as much of the truth as we know?" Dad asks. "Ber always does best when we trust her with as much information as she can handle."

"But how much is that?" Mom's voice is strained, and I think she might be crying, and whatever she says after that is too muffled to hear. But the next words she says are loud and clear. "I just don't want her to give up. On herself."

And my pump picks that moment to remind me of its low battery. Loudly. And repeatedly. I try to smother the buzzing, but I'm leaning against the railing and it's like the wood acts as an amplifier.

Dad rounds the corner first, looking up at me, his bushy eyebrows pulled together in a question.

"Morning," I say. My voice is too bright. But I'm not the one who should feel guilty. Yes, I was eavesdropping, which isn't great. But they were the ones talking behind my back. Keeping secrets.

"Is that a sweater or a straitjacket?" Dad jokes, coming up the last few steps to help disentangle me from the sweater.

"Feels more like a Collapse demon mid-smashing," I say, and Dad laughs as he helps me get my arms through the proper holes. "Thanks," I say as we walk to the kitchen together, where Clío chomps away at a bowl of food by the back door while Frangi and Mars eye her from the windowsill, tails twitching, waiting for an opportunity to steal some of her dog food even though they have perfectly good cat food of their own on top of the fridge.

Mom's back is to me, and I swear I see her wipe a tear away as she turns, smile bright, pointing to the plate of breakfast she's made me for: eggs, toast, and an apple.

"I need to charge my pump," I say, settling onto a stool and pulling the plate toward me.

"Oh, right." Mom's voice is tight. Yep, she was definitely crying. Her eyes are swollen too, and her cheeks are flushed. One of the Crowley curses: we can't really mask our emotions; our rosy cheeks and pale skin always give us away. Mom turns, wiping her eyes one more time as she searches for the pump charge cord in the drawer that's been assigned to my diabetes supplies.

I can't tell if they know I was listening, but as I stare at my breakfast, I just feel so overwhelmed and frustrated.

"Could I stay home today?" I ask.

"Why?" Mom asks as she emerges from the drawer with the cord. "I need to find the little thingy that connects to the wall and then we'll get you all charged up. But are you feeling okay?"

"Not really," I say. "I think the low yesterday at Phoebe's and nightmares last night—"

"Again?" Dad asks.

I'd forgotten I'd told him about my nightmares last week, before the Blood Moon ritual. I feel like I'm losing track of everything, that my whole life is just spiraling out of control in a way I'll never be able to get back on track.

"I'm just overwhelmed," I mutter as I stir my eggs around my plate instead of eating them. I see the look my parents exchange, but I pretend not to. Good, let them feel sorry for me. If it means I can stay home, I'm willing to endure their pity. Which feels dramatic, even in my own head. But my life has been pretty darn dramatic lately.

"Sure, yeah," Dad says. "I'll call the office and let them know we're keeping you home today."

"Thanks." I smile at him as he pulls out his phone and walks to the living room, leaving Mom and me alone.

Her lips twitch as she pours water over a tea bag and for a long moment it seems like she's going to say something. And then I feel my lips twitching too. I'm so much like her, but so different too. Dad's right, it's always been more Grandma Orla and me than Mom and me. Mom and I are still close, but it's felt like there's this fuzziness between us since Grandma Orla's been gone.

"I can make you something else," Mom says, looking down at my plate, where I've just been smooshing the eggs around.

"I'm just not really that hungry." I shrug. "Maybe I could just have something else a little later?"

"I really think you should have something—" she starts, but a loud buzzing interrupts us. At first, I think it's my pump again. But it's Mom's phone in her pocket as she leans against the counter. She pulls it out and mouths *I'm gonna take this really quick* like I'm her coworker and we're in an office TV show or something. But I take advantage of her distraction and Dad talking to the school in the other room. I grab the charge cord for my pump, abandon my breakfast, and head back upstairs to my room, Clío, Mars, and Frangi hot on my heels.

Now I'm the one ghosting Cai. For real this time. I don't even have a good excuse, other than being really, really mad at him. And at kind of the whole world. Wow, I'm being as dramatic as Maeve.

Which is almost enough of a reason to finally turn my phone back on and *not* fully ghost my boyfriend. Almost.

I just want a few minutes to sort through my own thoughts. But everything is so tangled up that my brain feels like a hairball. Well, a ball of hair, not the cat kind of hairball. Though maybe that too. Because my brain feels gross and soggy and slow.

I roll to grab my book and stop when I feel my insulin pump tug. I freeze, and it's like my body is back on the roof of Phoebe's house, the vines snaking away with my pump as it rips from my skin. But it's not ripped out, it's just pulling. Because I'm plugged into the wall. I'd completely forgotten I was charging the dang thing.

I grab a pillow, shove my face into it, and scream. Not too loud. I don't want Mom or Dad to come running in and think something is actually wrong. Even though it absolutely is.

Diabetes takes up so much of my brain. It's completely unfair. Maybe if I didn't have to think about my blood sugars and keeping my pump charged and having snacks with me, I'd be able to figure out how to get Grandma Orla back.

It's like diabetes has stolen half of my brain along with my entire pancreas.

And that's the final straw. Diabetes is a total bummer, but I can't let it take everything from me. I won't. I'm going to figure this out. I'm going to get Grandma Orla and Fin back. And if I can't trust my friends or parents or sister to help me, I'm just going to have to do it myself.

CHAPTER FOURTEEN

sometimes you just have to do it yourself

Once the idea takes root in my brain, it spreads like . . . something that grows really fast. I don't really know that much about plants. Which makes me think of Phoebe and yesterday and, just, nope. I'm not going there. I'm going forward. I want to be a person whose brain is mostly looking to the future instead of the past. And right now, I can just *feel* a plan coming together.

Because that's what finally clicked into place in the midst of my epic pity party: we haven't actually tried anything. We've talked about clues and magical theories and riddles and spells. But we haven't tried conjuring another Mystery demon. Well, ideally the same Mystery demon.

And that's what I'm going to do. I'm just going to conjure Fin again.

Maybe it's that simple.

Fin always said a hundred words when just a few would do the trick, so maybe their prophecy was just an epic pep talk.

I think of the final lines:

Find your story—the thread only you can weave in the tapestry of magic. But it must be true. Only then will you find us. Only then will you bring her home.

I was the first witch to bind a Mystery demon in generations. The first since my great-great-grandma. And what's truer than my need to get Grandma Orla and Fin back?

The spell Maeve and I used to bind Fin was pretty simple. So I'll keep it simple this time too. My stomach clenches as I grab a pen and paper and my glucose meter. It clenches so bad it actually hurts. That's okay though. I'm just nervous.

"Nerves aren't always bad," Grandma Orla always says. "Sometimes they just teach you what you're ready for." And I'm ready to do something. Samhain is only a week away, and I want Grandma Orla back where she belongs before then. Here. With us. In this dimension.

Methinks the little witch doth protest too much, Fin's voice says in my mind. And it's so clear and so snarky that I look around the room, half expecting them to be here already. But it's just the version of Fin that lives in my memory.

No. Looking forward. Moving forward.

I decide to lay out Fin's Prophecy and the original binding spell side by side.

Fin's Prophecy	Binding Spell
The key is the story you tell yourself. About who you are and who you may become.	A simple task to complete, Given purpose, what a treat. Do your job, make it right,
Lives are stories. Rooted in the telling, but also changed. Clutched too tightly, stories cannot grow. And grow they must. And what story isn't made better for a bit of mystery? Question asked together, spoken aloud, or held silently in our hearts keep us connected. Find your story—the thread only you can weave in the tapestry of magic. But it must be true. Only then will you find us. Only then will you bring her home.	Balance sought, blood just right. Use the scent to show the way, Highs and lows are kept at bay. Balance is what must be found, What does Bernadette Crowley need now?

I stare at all the words, my certainty seeping out of me like air out of a leaky bike tire. But then I reread the first line. The key is the story I tell myself. I'm going to tell myself the version of my story where I get Fin and Grandma Orla back.

Clío and Mars jump up onto the bed, almost in unison. Clío slips a little and I catch her, hauling her up, and Mars paces over and paws the pieces of paper where I've written the spell and the prophecy.

"You guys are gonna help, right?" I ask. And I know they can't understand me like they can understand Cai, but I can tell they agree. "Should we go to Grandma Orla's?"

Clío votes no by pacing in a little circle and plopping down on the bed.

"No, yeah, you're right. If this is about the thread only I can weave, I should just do it right here, in my room."

I grab my pen and paper and pull out my phone. I was going to open iDemon and start searching for the best spell to tinker with, but that would mean turning my phone on. Which would mean seeing Cai's texts. Because let's be real, I would look.

The ache in my stomach doubles, but so does my need to see this through.

The spell to bind Fin wasn't meant to bind them, but it did. And it was pretty simple. The power in my blood and the power of my name is what did the trick. That and the question.

I scribble down a few notes:

> Include a question.
> Keep it simple.
> Get Fin, not just some rando Mystery.

The last part feels like the trickiest, so I start there. Grandma Orla always says to start with complexity and work your way back to simple.

I read the second-to-last line of the prophecy again.

> *Questions asked together, spoken aloud, or held silently in our hearts keep us connected.*

What is the question held silently in my heart? What is the question that connects Fin and me? There are so many. There are a thousand things I didn't get to ask them, and hundreds I did that they left without answers.

But then I really think about our days together, and about all their philosophizing and all of Grandma Orla's secrecy and rules, and also her fierceness and Fin's stubbornness. And when I think about it more, and about the absolutely bonkers idea that Fin was bound to my great-great-grandma once, almost a hundred years ago, the question clicks into place in my chest.

It's almost a physical thing, the words coming together just so. And I know the words are special and important.

I know they are the start of a spell that's never been cast before.

What stories are Ber and Fin weaving?

"Is this what it's like for Maeve when she finds the anchor to an amazing new spell?" I ask Mars. He just purrs at me and lies down across the original binding spell. I'm going to take that as a yes.

And then it's like the ideas start coming through me, not even from me, and I race to write down the spell as fast as I can. Maybe I'm being silly, but maybe Fin is sending it to me somehow, because it feels like magic the way the spell falls together. Simple but complex. Mysterious but grounded. It's perfect.

I laugh a little. I'm giddy. Why didn't I think of this weeks ago? It's been so obvious this whole time.

I'm the witch with powerful blood. I'm the bearer of my great-great-grandma's name. I'm the youngest in a line of witches whose history can be traced to the discovery of blood magic. I don't need anyone else. Other people just disappoint you and complicate things. They bring their own problems and ideas and prejudices.

Once I put the finishing touches on the spell and read through it a couple of times, I start setting the scene. I put any dirty clothes that were lingering on the floor into the hamper and straighten the books on my desk. I put all the wrappers from the gummies I ate two nights ago when my blood sugar was low in the trash bin. I'm about to make my bed when I stop.

No. Part of my magic is my messiness. My imperfections. What was it that Fin said right before I unbound them?

Thank you for being brave, strong, and out-of-control enough to let me through the Veil and into your life.

I'm not looking for perfection. This isn't Maeve's spell. Or Mom's. Or even Grandma Orla's. It's mine. And it's messy and imperfect but so totally me. And so is my room. And my dog. And my kitten.

"Okay, Mars, you come over here, please." I point to what I'm pretty sure is the eastern side of my bedroom. Incredibly, my kitten listens and leaps from the bed and settles right where I've pointed.

"Okay, Clío, you here," I say, pointing to the opposite side of the room. She misunderstands at first, looking at my hand like I'm waiting for her to alert, but I've checked my CGM reading twice. I'm hovering in the 180s. A little bit high, but better than a little bit low. Eventually I coax Clío into place and convince her to stay put as I grab the pitch-black candle Grandma Orla gave me for my birthday. She said I was supposed to save it for my first big conjuring. I'm pretty sure this is not what I had in mind, but it feels right to me.

I find a box of matches in my desk drawer that has exactly one match left. I don't have many conjuring tools that aren't my lancet in here, I realize. Probably because I'm absolutely not supposed to be doing any intentional unaccompanied conjurings, never mind a binding slash rescue mission. But I'm done playing by anyone's rules except my own.

My hands are shaking as I settle between Mars and Clío. My spell is set in front of me. My lancet is placed beside it. The candle lights quickly and burns a bright, eerie purple. I take a deep breath, pick up my lancet, and brace myself to start the spell.

The knock on my door startles me so bad that I jump, tipping over the candle. I reach out and grab it just in time, righting it before it can light Mars's super fluffy tail on fire. Which would absolutely *not* be the right vibe for our reunion with Fin and Grandma Orla.

"All okay, Ber?" Mom's voice slices through the door and I freeze.

"Yeah, just reading," I say quickly.

"I was thinking of going and grabbing us some breakfast sandwiches and London Fogs from City Brew," she says. "Do you want to come?"

"Is it okay if I stay here?" I ask. I wince, letting out a hiss of pain as some wax drips onto my hand. I hadn't realized I was still holding the candle that almost toppled into Mars.

Clío trots over to me, stepping on the perfectly placed spell.

"Of course," Mom says. "I'll get you egg and cheese on a pretzel bun?"

"Perfect," I say. *Please just leave, please just leave, please just leave*, I chant to myself in my head as I hold my breath. My eyes are glued to the doorknob, waiting for it to turn. Waiting for Mom to waltz into the room and ruin everything with her worry.

"Dad's downstairs making a pie with the apples Maeve and Tempest picked this weekend," Mom says. "Just call down if you need anything, okay, sweetie?"

"Thanks, Mom," I say. And then wait to hear her footsteps walk away. When they don't, I add, "I love you."

"Love you too, sweetheart. So much. I'll be back soon."

And then the floorboards creak and I hear her walking down the stairs.

"That was close," I say to Mars as he glares at Clío. My incredible kitten held formation that entire time, and he needs me to understand that it makes him superior to my less disciplined dog.

"Just a few weeks ago, you were the one breaking formation," I remind Mars in a whisper as I direct Clío back to her place.

Okay, I can do this. I jump again when I hear a

rumbling from downstairs, but it's just the garage door opening. Mom's gone. Dad's distracted. Now is the perfect time.

I take one more deep breath, readjust my lancet in my left hand, ready to prick my ring finger on my right hand. And then I start my spell.

CHAPTER FIFTEEN

a witch and her mystery

A question that bears repeating
While searching for hidden meanings—
Now bring us the clue
And bind us like glue
For a witch and her mystery
Are bound throughout history—
What stories are Ber and Fin weaving?

I feel the words vibrate in my chest as I cast the spell. I use my lancet to pierce my finger as I say my name and again as I say Fin's. I let one drop of blood fall onto the spell and another into the flame of the candle. Which goes out as the drop of blood smothers the flame.

It's the middle of the morning, so the candle going

out can't be what changes the light in the room. But the light in the room does change. It gets darker, as if a mist has smothered the light from the window. No, that's actually mist. In my room. And it's getting thicker.

Clío whines and scurries across the room, curling up in my lap just as the mist becomes so thick that I can barely see the spell on the floor in front of me. My heart races with equal parts hope and fear. Because this has to mean the spell worked, right? I've never seen anything like this before. Never *felt* anything like this before. I jump and let out a little squeak of pain as Mars lands on my shoulder, his claws cutting right through my sweater and finding my skin.

And then a low, lilting voice swears.

In Irish.

"Fin?" I ask. Too loudly, but I almost don't even care. Because the spell worked. "Grandma Orla?" I add. I blink into the mist, which seems to be clearing. A figure is sitting in my desk chair. But only one. Oh no, did Fin leave Grandma Orla in the demon dimension?

"Where in all the dimensions are we?" the figure asks. And my heart sinks, because it's not Fin. I've had their cobblestone voice in my head for weeks and whoever this is has a similar accent, but I know it's not them. It's not Fin.

What have I done?

Who have I conjured?

Or bound?

"Are you a Mystery?" I ask, my voice small and scared, and suddenly I really, *really* wish Mom were home.

"I've been called worse," the voice answers. And the mist is finally cleared enough that the figure comes into focus. It's a . . . little old man? A really handsome little old man, but that is definitely a human sitting at my desk. A tiny black fluff ball is perched in his lap. When the man meets my gaze, his pale blue eyes widen, and his mouth falls open like a startled character in a cartoon. "Are you . . ." He trails off, running a trembling hand over the black fluff ball's back before he swallows and starts again. "Are you . . . a Crowley?"

And now it's my turn for my jaw to pop open like a cartoon. How does this man know my name? And how did he get here?

"Did I conjure you?" I ask.

"Are you capable of conjuring witches?" he asks.

And he may not be Fin, but he sure is matching the Fin vibes with all these questions.

We stare at each other in silence for a long moment, the last of the mist disappearing from my bedroom. Clío rises from my lap and walks toward the man, taking an exploratory sniff at his shoes. They are leather and look as old as he does. His pants also look old-fashioned, and he wears a deep blue knit sweater and a little cap with a flat bill, white hair spilling out of the sides.

"Are you from the past?" The question is out of my mouth before I can register how ridiculous it is.

The man laughs so hard the ball of fluff jumps from his lap, startling Clío, who backs away so fast she whacks me in the face with her tail. The ball of fluff reveals itself to be a tiny black cat with a smushed face and little folded ears. It hisses at Clío before jumping up onto my desk.

"Now I know I'm not as young as I once was, but accusing me of being a historical artifact is a bit harsh." The man pulls his cap off, leaning forward in the chair—*my* chair. "I was mid-conjuring, a rather impressive Direct who was supposed to be taking me to my grandson's cottage for tea, when I was suddenly deposited in this chair, along with half the cloud Nimby and I were traveling through."

"So you're a blood witch?" I ask.

"Among other things," he answers. "And you're definitely a Crowley."

"How do I keep conjuring people who already know who I am?" I mutter as Mars leaps off my shoulder, determined to inspect the newly arrived cat.

"Keep conjuring?" the man asks. "Do you make conjuring people a habit?" He pauses and then leans so far forward he's perched on the very edge of my chair, and it looks like he might fall right off it, sucked forward by his curiosity. "And can you teach me how?"

"Probably not," I say. "I was trying for—" I break off. I was just about to spill the beans and tell this complete stranger that I was trying to bind a Mystery demon. Again. When he's clearly a blood witch. And Irish. He's probably even more old-school than Grandma Orla. I need to figure out who he is and get rid of him as soon as possible. "Well, I was trying for something else," I finish in a whisper. "And it would be great if you could just tell me who you are and then . . . leave." Well, that wasn't as impressive or commanding as I wanted it to be.

The man frowns for a long time, or maybe just a couple of seconds but it feels like a long time because in the silence I can hear Dad singing downstairs. Maybe I should shout down to him. There's a strange old man in my bedroom. Granted, I did seem to bring him here. Somehow. But what if Dad attacks him or something? I think about Mom nearly setting a Mayhem demon on Cai at the Blood Moon ritual last week. He's just a little old man. I don't want unintentional grandpa murder on my conscience. Unless he does something creepy. But so far, he's just sat there and asked questions. He seems harmless enough.

"Names hold power," the man finally says. "I think you should offer up yours first in a fair trade."

"Are you sure you're not a Mystery demon in disguise or something?" I grumble, hugging Clío to my chest.

"A Mystery demon?" the man asks. "Now how would a young witch like yourself know about Mystery demons? I thought they were keeping such things from the youngins these days. Particularly if we're on the North American continent, as your accent and striking resemblance to Orla Crowley suggests."

"You know my grandma?" I ask.

"As I suspected," the man says, smiling and leaning back in the chair, crossing his arms over his chest. "You must be Maeve . . . or not, wait." He taps a finger on his lips, and I see a claddagh ring on the ring finger of his right hand. It looks just like the one Grandma Orla keeps in a little box on her bedside table. "You must be Bernadette," he says, and I'm sure my face gives away that he's right. But I don't even care because I think I've figured out who he is.

Irish. Old, like *as old as Grandma Orla* old. Not *just* a blood witch.

"And you're Patrick Walsh."

CHAPTER SIXTEEN
classic crowley magic

The look on Patrick Walsh's face tells me everything I need to know. Well, not exactly *everything*. I need to know a heck of a lot more things right about now. But his narrowed eyes and crooked little almost-smile tell me a lot. Namely that he's definitely Patrick Walsh. Which means . . .

"You're Grandma Orla's nemesis," I whisper.

"Nemesis is rather dramatic, don't you think?" Patrick asks.

"It sounds like you've earned the title," I say, pushing myself off the floor finally. My stomach is tied in horrible knots, and I don't want to be looking up at this little old man whose name Grandma Orla practically considers a curse. I want to look him straight in the eye when I ask him what in the demon dimension he's doing here. And so, I sit on the edge of my bed and lean forward to put my elbows on my knees like cops do in interrogation scenes. At least on TV. But as my weight shifts on my bed, the plushies piled in the corner tumble down around me, completely ruining the intimidation vibes I was going for.

"Well, if this is the welcome I'm going to receive when *you* were the one who somehow brought me here, I think I'll be on my way." Patrick stands, scoops the tiny black cat off the stack of books it's settled on, and pulls his dagger out from under his sweater. "How far from Kerry are we exactly?" he asks.

"About 4,240 miles," I answer automatically. It's a number I have seared into my brain by Grandma Orla. "You'll need multiple Directs for the journey back. We usually just take a plane."

"Amadán," Patrick says. "Then you'll just have to send me back. However you got me here."

"Ummm . . . I was obviously not expecting you," I say. "I don't think we want to risk that. And I've already done one experimental spell today, I think you'll just have to—"

"Say more about this experimental spell," Patrick says, cutting me off. "Is that it?" He points to the spell. Where I left it on the floor next to the extinguished black candle and my lancet.

Before I can answer, he's scooped it up and I watch his Paul Hollywood–level blue eyes scan the lines, getting wider and wider as they move down the page.

"Well, this is an interesting little spell you've crafted here," he says. And I brace myself for the scolding. I think I even physically wince, imagining what Grandma Orla or Mom would say. What they *will* say. How much trouble I'm going to be in when they find out. But Patrick's next question chases the impending consequences from my brain completely.

"Did you intend to use weather magic in this spell? It's rather ingenious, but unexpected from a Crowley. Though truly clever, which is classic Crowley magic. In fact—"

But I jump to my feet, waving my arms and making shushing sounds as I rush to my door. Because the singing downstairs has stopped, and I can definitely hear footsteps coming up the stairs. Patrick starts to talk again, but before he can get a word out, I whirl around, channel Grandma Orla, and fix him with what I hope is a withering stare.

Infuriatingly, he smiles! But he shrugs and pretends to zip his mouth shut. I glare at him for another second before I turn back to the door, take a deep breath, and stick my head out into the hallway.

"Ber! Did you smell the pie?" Dad asks. His smile takes over his whole face and my brain screams *don't be suspicious* as I try to make my face look as delighted by pie as I can muster. My stomach growls, which helps add to the realism.

"It smells great, Dad," I say. "I'll come down and have a slice in just a few minutes, okay?"

"Sounds good, kiddo," Dad says. "I'm gonna switch into sweats. Hard pants aren't pie appropriate, you know?"

"True facts," I say. "Don't eat the whole thing before Mom and I get some."

"No promises," he says with a laugh as he walks past me and disappears into his and Mom's room, humming the theme song to a Marvel TV show I can't quite place. I wait a few seconds and then pull my head back into my room and spin back to the first human conjuring in the history of blood magic.

"Well, that would help explain the power of your spell," Patrick says in a hushed whisper as I close the door behind me.

I turn around to see what Patrick's staring at. His cheeks slightly pink, an apologetic smile on his wrinkled face as he looks at my bed. And when I see what he sees, my cheeks burst into flame too. Actually, my entire body feels like I've been thrown into a bonfire of embarrassment. Because there's a red patch of blood on the bed exactly where I was sitting.

The twisting in my stomach wasn't just nerves. It was cramps.

I just got my very first period.

CHAPTER SEVENTEEN
un-brie-lievable circumstances

The stream of curses that leaves my mouth would make Grandma Orla proud. Patrick Walsh's bushy white eyebrows get higher and higher on his face, but he doesn't say anything else. I have no clue what to do. I feel so ridiculous. And before I can stop them, tears pool in my eyes and spill down my cheeks as I stand frozen, staring at the bloodstain on the bed. I was expecting this. Eventually. Soon, even. Maeve got her first period when she was thirteen and I'm almost thirteen and a half. And it's not like I'm squeamish about blood or periods. But it just feels like one more thing, one more inconvenient, frustrating, bloody thing. And I have too many things already. I'm buried in things, and I don't think I can take any more.

I didn't notice myself falling to the floor until Patrick

is kneeling before me and Clío is forcing her way into my lap. All I can think about is how I can now feel the wetness, how it's probably still seeping through my pants and getting all over the floor.

"I give up," I say. And I'm fully crying into Clío's fur and she's so confused. And I wish Cai were here to explain this to her, but I've also never been more glad that Cai isn't here. Because he'd be so chill about this. I know it. And that makes it worse somehow. "I just want her back," I whisper. And I feel like a whiny little kid. But this moment was supposed to be sacred and special. Grandma Orla and Mom threw Maeve a party. Periods are powerful for blood witches. Period blood doesn't conjure anything, thank the goddess. But it supercharges your conjurings. If a menstruating witch is present, they always lead the big holiday spells.

This isn't how this was supposed to happen. I don't want it to happen this way.

"Want who back?" Patrick asks, his voice gentle as he just sits with me on the floor of my room while Mars and his fluffy black kitten blink down at us from the windowsill and my bedside table. And I figure things can't really get any worse, so I just decide to tell him.

"Grandma Orla," I say. "Orla Crowley. She's in the demon dimension with a Mystery named Finley Mac-Intire and the spell was me trying to get them back."

Patrick's fuzzy white caterpillar eyebrows rise so far

up his forehead they meld with the hair sticking out of his cap, but he just nods twice. Then he asks, "And I take it this is your first visit from the blood fairy?"

I nod.

"Well, that's a lot for one young witch to handle."

I let out a stuttering breath as I nod again. Clío pushes her soft snoot into my cheek, and I smile as she starts licking away my tears. Then I notice my pump vibrating in my pocket, so I hold out my hand and Clío stops licking my tears long enough to alert that my blood sugar is high. Because of course it is.

I pull out my pump, and Patrick's lips tighten into a thin line.

"And you're a diabetic?" he asks, and shakes his head when I nod as I confirm a correction bolus for my blood sugar, which is now 249. "A diabetic and a blood witch? That sounds extra complicated. I've never actually heard of a blood witch with diabetes."

"I'm a bit of a mess," I say. "I mean, on a good day, and this is not a good day. In case that wasn't super obvious."

"I might have been able to use some context clues to deduce as much," Patrick says with a kind smile. And it's hard to imagine him as anyone's nemesis, especially not Grandma Orla's. There's something about him that actually reminds me of her.

"Ber?" Dad's voice calls from downstairs.

I crack the door open. "Yeah?" I ask.

"We're out of ice cream," he shouts up to me. "I'm just gonna go raid Orla's freezer and see if she's got any stashed away."

My heart clenches at the thought of us eating Grandma Orla's ice cream without her, but that's the least of my worries right now and getting Dad out of the house for a few minutes seems ideal.

"Sounds gouda," I call back.

"Gouda?" Patrick asks in a whisper.

"Like good," I explain. "But make it cheese."

"Un-Brie-lievable." He shakes his head, but mirth dances in his eyes at his own cheese pun. "That was your father, I imagine?"

"Yeah. He made a pie," I explain.

"I heard that part," Patrick says. "Smells like apple."

The door closes downstairs, and I push myself off the ground. I can't help glancing at the floor and I'm relieved to see that there's no obvious bloodstain there.

"Okay, this is maybe going to sound really batty," I begin, and when Patrick doesn't interrupt, I keep going. "But here's the thing. I'm going to need to deal with this whole period situation before I deal with the whole *you* situation. And I have a feeling my spell brought you here for a reason, so can you just . . . chill for a bit?"

"Chill?" He pushes himself off the ground with surprising agility for someone so ancient.

"Yeah, like, hang out in here with the little cat until I can figure out what to do with you," I say as I gather up the candle and spell and shove them into my bedside table drawer and throw a pillow over the bloodstain on my duvet.

"Do with me?" Patrick asks as he scoops his cat into his arms.

"Okay, bad choice of words," I say. "But I'm dealing with a very stressful situation right now."

"You're not wrong about that," Patrick agrees.

"Could you just stay up here out of sight until I can make a plan?" I ask as I grab a change of clothes and retrieve my phone from under my pillow.

"Well, you're most definitely Orla's granddaughter, that's for sure," Patrick grumbles, but he settles down into my desk chair again and pulls my biology textbook off my desk and starts leafing through it. "Nimby and I will endeavor to chill." He nods at the cat, who blinks its bright golden eyes at me.

"Great," I say. "Just, be silent, okay?"

He nods and doesn't say anything. Which I guess is exactly what I asked him to do.

And as me and Clío make our way across the hall and into the bathroom I can't help feeling like maybe Patrick

Walsh is part Mystery demon. Because this feels like Fin all over again. But it's precisely that feeling that makes me want to keep him around long enough to find out why he landed in my room when I tried to bring Fin back. And Patrick says there was weather magic in my spell. How could I even have done that if Fin weren't helping me somehow?

A bajillion questions race through my mind as I turn on my phone. There are seventeen texts from Cai and twenty-nine in a new group chat he's started with me and Phoebe. But I ignore them all.

"Siri, call Mom," I say.

She picks up on the second ring.

"Everything okay?"

"I . . ." My voice shakes and I almost dissolve into tears again, but I don't want her to freak out and think that something's actually really wrong. Like, diabetes wrong. So I blurt out the truth as quickly as I can. Well, the part she needs to know. "I got my period. I'm in the upstairs bathroom and—"

"I'm almost home," she says immediately, not even letting me finish. "Sit tight and I'll be there in less than five minutes."

And she's back home, up the stairs, and in the bathroom hugging me tight in three minutes and twenty-one seconds. Not that I was counting.

CHAPTER EIGHTEEN
the blood fairy

Mom hugs me for a long time. Before she says anything. Before she does anything else. She just kneels down next to the toilet and hugs me. And I hug her back so hard I feel like we both might just smush together permanently. But that would be terrible, actually. Basically, it's a super great hug. And I didn't know how much I needed it.

"How are you feeling?" Mom asks.

"I don't even know," I mumble into her shoulder. "But this explains a lot."

She laughs and hugs me even harder before she sits back on her heels and takes my hands in hers.

"I'm not going to do any of that becoming a woman stuff because we know that's nonsense," she says. "But this is a big change, especially for your magic and for your diabetes. I want you to be extra careful over the next few days and I'm so glad you stayed home. Good instincts." She sighs, pressing her lips together, and she seems to be trying to make up her mind about something.

"I'm really glad you have your CGM now," she says finally. "I was worried we were rushing into that a bit, but I need you to be extra careful the next few days. All blood witches have increased power when they are on their cycle. And we've seen how powerful your blood can be, even when you're trying not to conjure." I see the worry flicker across her face as we both think of all the accidentals I conjured my first month back at school. "I think it would actually be best if you don't test unless absolutely necessary," she adds. "And no official conjurings either. We'll do a controlled experiment on day two or three of your cycle, with both Dad and me there to supervise, okay?"

I nod. Because I have to agree. But secretly my mind is racing, wondering if maybe some extra power is exactly what I need to make the spell work if I try again. And I feel a tiny bit guilty about kind-of sort-of lying to her until I remember the conversation I overheard earlier this morning.

Mom smiles and squeezes my hands and starts to pull

things out from under the sink. And I know about pads and tampons. I know Maeve uses period undies instead. But it's one thing to know it and another to need it.

"And no wonder you had nightmares," Mom says after we decide to stick to pads for today at least. "I always have nightmares when the blood fairy is visiting. Maeve does too."

"Well, I don't love that for us," I say, and Mom laughs. And it's so nice to make her laugh. It feels like we haven't laughed enough in the last month. But then I realize that's because of me. Because I'm the one who can't let myself laugh because I miss Grandma Orla too much. And as my laughter fizzles out, two emotions I've been much more used to lately come rushing back: frustration and anger.

"There's another reason I wanted to stay home," I say. Mom frowns at me from where she's perched on the edge of the bathtub, but she doesn't interrupt, so I keep going. "I overheard you and Dad talking. This morning. I know I shouldn't have been listening, but I heard you talking about me, and about Grandma Orla, and what aren't you telling me? What did you find in Grandma Orla's books?"

Mom sighs and looks down at her hands for a long time before she answers.

"I'm sorry you had to hear that, Ber. I thought you

might have heard part of it, but I promise we're not keeping—"

"Mom, please, just tell me what you found in Grandma Orla's books," I plead.

"Nothing," Mom says, still looking at her hands.

"Mom, seriously!" I screech, and I want to launch myself across the bathroom and shake her. Why can't she just tell me the truth for once?

"No, Ber, that's what I'm trying to tell you." Mom looks up at me and the sadness in her eyes makes my throat tight. "I've been looking and looking, and I haven't found anything." And then tears fill her eyes, and I would give anything for her to stop talking.

I take it back, I want to shout. *I don't want to know. I don't want you to say what you're about to say.*

But then she says it anyway.

"I don't think there's a way to bring her back."

"No, Mom, don't say that."

"See? Ber, this is exactly why I didn't want to—"

"No, you can't be giving up," I say, cutting her off.

"I'm so sorry, Ber," Mom says. And there's a finality in her voice that feels like a knife right into my heart.

"You're giving up on her," I say. And I almost wish I were crying. But I feel numb. This feels worse than when she went through the Tairseach in the first place. Because she did that to save us. And now Mom isn't even going to try to save her.

"I'm not, Ber," Mom says. "I promise I'm not, but—"

And I stop listening. I can't listen. I don't want to hear all her excuses. How many books she looked through. How many spells she considered. How there's a reason witches don't move between dimensions.

"I'm sorry I didn't tell you before, Ber," Mom says. "But you are dealing with so much and I didn't want to disappoint you."

"Disappoint me?" I splutter. Because that's the understatement of all understatements. "I'm not disappointed, I'm—" But I break off, because there isn't a word in the English language for how much this hurts. But I bet Grandma Orla would know one in Irish, and Fin would definitely know one.

"Please don't give up on her," I say instead. "On them."

"I'm not," Mom says. "I won't. But I just need your focus to be on things in this dimension, okay? Your magic is already complicated, and so is your diabetes, and your period is only going to make that harder. I promise I just want what's best for you."

And I almost argue. I almost tell her I just accidentally conjured a witch from across the world. That he's sitting in my room right now. And that I brought part of a cloud with him. And if I can do that, maybe I really can get Grandma Orla and Fin back too.

But I see the way her chin juts out, the exact way it does when she's arguing with Grandma Orla. The exact way it does when Maeve has stretched her curfew to its absolute limit. She's not budging on this, not because she can't. But because she doesn't want to.

"I love you so much, Ber," Mom says, pulling me to my feet and hugging me again. And I let her hug me and try not to feel like she's lying.

Mom goes back downstairs after hugging me at least five more times. There was a second where I thought she was going to insist on coming into my room with me, but once I hear her and Dad talking downstairs, I relax. A tiny bit. I still have to deal with Patrick. And by deal with, I mean convince him to help me figure out this spell because obviously I can't tell Mom.

But when I get back to my room, Patrick's gone.

"Patrick?" I whisper as I shut my door behind me. "Patrick, where are you?"

There's no reply. I look in my closet and under my bed as my heart starts to race. Did he leave? Could he have conjured a Movement demon and left without me or Mom noticing?

I look out the window and peer down into the yard. And that's when I see it. Grandma Orla's door opens and then closes. All by itself. But not before a tiny black cat scurries across the threshold.

CHAPTER NINETEEN

jumping to conclusions

It takes a few hours of eating pie and pretending not to be furious with Mom before I can sneak away to Grandma Orla's. The eating pie part wasn't so bad—Dad's really good at pies—but the pretending not to be mad at Mom part was almost impossible. So between my cramping belly and frayed nerves, I'm exhausted by the time I cross Grandma Orla's small porch and creep into her house.

I left Clío in the house, but Mars and Frangi couldn't be dissuaded from joining me. Dogs are much better at listening to what you tell them than cats.

"I gathered the house was unused," Patrick says as soon as I close the door behind me. Which makes me jump even though I was expecting to find him in here.

"This is not what I meant by chill," I say. "But I'm glad you didn't decide to Direct demon your way back to Ireland, because I think I need your help."

"What exactly can I help you with that your own family can't?" he asks. "And what makes you think that I will help? The Crowleys haven't been altogether kind to the Walshes since your grandmother—" He breaks off.

"Since my grandmother what?" I ask.

"Well, I'm sure you know her side of the story," he says.

"That's exactly why I hope you might help me," I say. "Because I want to get my grandma back so I can tell her how wrong she was. About you, and about a lot of other things too."

I don't know exactly why I say that. But it feels true in the same way the spell did.

"I can't explain it," I say. "I just can feel that I can trust you. I think Fin sent you to me."

"And Fin is the Mystery demon you mentioned before?" Patrick asks. And there's a little hiccup in his voice when he says *Mystery*.

"I'll tell you if you at least agree to hear me out," I say, holding out a hand for him to shake. He pauses for a second, but then he takes it. "And," I add quickly. "You will stay back here in Grandma Orla's house and not give me away to my parents."

He purses his lips and his eyebrows squish together for a second, but then he nods and shakes my hand.

"However," he says, stopping mid-shake. "You do not yet appear to be initiated, and though I'm curious to hear what kind of magic you're attempting to get up to, and I'm more eager than most to have an opportunity to tell Orla Crowley—to her face—that she's wrong about something, I reserve the right to at least pretend to be a responsible adult and put a stop to all of this."

"Deal," I say quickly. "Because you're not going to want to."

"I respect the confidence," Patrick says. "Now, what's your pitch?"

I lead the way into Grandma Orla's study and settle down with her greatest nemesis to make a new plan for how to rescue her from the demon dimension. You know, just a normal, ordinary Monday when you're a diabetic blood witch.

I've told Patrick almost everything about what went down in September and I'm about to tell him about Fin's Prophecy when there's a frantic knock on Grandma Orla's front door.

"Stay here," I hiss. "And leave the lights off," I add when I notice how dark it's gotten. But then I pause, because why is someone knocking on Grandma Orla's door? If it were Mom or Dad or Maeve, they would have just used the hidden key and barged in. And thank goodness they didn't. So, who is it?

That question is answered almost as soon as I think it by Cai's voice calling through the door.

"Ber, please, open up! Quick!"

I scramble for the lock on the door. The second I get it unlocked and swing the door open Cai rushes through, Phoebe hot on his heels.

"Close it, close it, close it!" Phoebe squeals.

"The birds are definitely from Fin," Cai says as I spot an entire flock of starlings swooping around the yard right before I slam the door shut.

"Ooh, did you get another cat?" Phoebe asks, scooping Patrick's tiny black cat into her arms before I can answer.

"She came with me, actually," Patrick says from the doorway.

"What's their name and are you Ber's grandpa?" Phoebe asks.

"Nimby, short for Nimbus," Patrick says. "And I might have been, if things had gone a bit differently between Orla and me."

"Wait, what?" I splutter.

"Well, if you're not related to Ber, why are you here?" Phoebe asks, crossing her arms over her chest as

I try to process what Patrick just implied about him and *my grandma*.

"I sort of conjured him," I explain.

"You can conjure people?" Phoebe asks.

"Not normally," I say. "But I guess I sort of hijacked his Direct demon or something? And I know it sounds bonkers, but I think Fin had something to do with it." Then I remember what Cai said as he ran through the door. "Wait, did you say you are certain the birds are from Fin? How?"

"Could we bring this chaotic but entertaining conversation back to the sitting room?" Patrick asks before Cai can explain. "My knees are not what they once were, and I've had a rather long and abrupt and slightly distressing journey."

"Did you say Nimbus, like the cloud?" Phoebe asks as we make our way back into Grandma Orla's study.

"Yes, indeed, young witch," Patrick says.

"Oh, I'm not a witch," Phoebe says. "Neither is he. We're mages."

"Ah, the young mages from Bernadette's dramatic tale, I take it?" he asks as he settles back into Grandma Orla's chair. I hope she'll forgive me for letting him sit there. She'll have to if he helps get her back to our dimension.

"Yes, this is Phoebe Fang and Cai Anderson," I say.

"Plant mage," Phoebe says.

"Mind mage," Cai says.

"Mind mage with another message from Fin?" I ask.

"Right, yes." Cai sits on the couch next to me while Phoebe settles on the ground with Mars and Frangi. "I drank the mugwort tea that Phoebe gave me last night," he explains. "And I dreamed about Fin and Orla. I think I saw the demon dimension."

"What?" My voice is so high I bet only bats and dogs can hear it. "Why didn't you tell me?"

"I did," Cai says. "I texted you like a million times."

"Oh, right." A pit of guilt forms in my stomach. "I had my phone off. I didn't really want to talk with you guys."

"We totally get that," Cai says. "And we wouldn't have come over without asking first if I didn't think you needed to hear what I saw and heard as soon as possible."

"Which was what?" I demand. I can't tell what the weird quality in Cai's voice is. "You're really starting to freak me out."

"So we've been focused on trying to decipher the clues the birds are sending me from Fin, right?" Cai asks.

I nod and make a *keep talking and get to the point faster* circle with my hand.

"Well, Orla and Fin weren't the only ones to go through that portal thingy," he says.

"Tairseach," Patrick corrects him, but then holds up

his hands palms out. "Sorry, sorry, I'm just still in a bit of shock about that part of Bernadette's tale. Go on."

"The Kalispell Coven," Cai says. "I saw them, surrounded by what I think were other Mystery demons. Their minds felt like Fin's anyway. And something was super, super wrong. And I think maybe they're . . . I don't know." He runs a hand through his hair, tugging it a little bit and grimacing. "I don't want to jump to any conclusions; it was just a dream, after all."

"I say jump," Phoebe says. "Mugwort dreams may be strange, but they don't lie."

"I think whatever the Kalispell Coven is doing in the demon dimension is hurting the Mystery demons," Cai says. "They looked like they were in pain. And then I saw Fin, and they weren't there, they were somewhere else, and it—" He breaks off and his face scrunches up before he sighs. "I think they were fighting with Orla. And it all just seemed super bad, and I just wonder if—" He breaks off again and I fight the urge to reach across the space between us and shake him until he says whatever it is he's afraid to say.

"I'm afraid to say it because it's scary," he says. And then he winces. "Sorry, I wasn't trying to—"

"Please, Cai, just spit it out," I say. I don't even care that he's reading my mind. Well, I sort of care, but his mind mage powers are coming in especially useful right now, so I don't care *too* much.

"I think we've been going about this all wrong," Cai says. "I think rather than getting Fin and Orla out of the demon dimension, I think they need our help. I think they need us to go into the demon dimension after them."

CHAPTER TWENTY

grandma orla's not so nemesis

"Now that is an interesting idea," Patrick says, while my brain is still fully buffering like some ancient internet connection.

"But the prophecy ends with 'only then will you bring her home,'" I say. "I thought—"

"We all did," Cai says. "I think your parents did too. But what if Fin didn't have all the information when they passed me the prophecy? They were thinking fast, worried about being ripped apart between dimensions. And their mind works so differently than ours—it's almost like they have a completely different kind of logic, if they have logic at all."

"That tracks," I say. "But why not just tell us?"

"Maybe they couldn't?" Phoebe offers with a shrug.

"Can I see this prophecy?" Patrick asks. "Or hear

it? Though I process information a bit better when it's written down, so a printed copy would be ideal."

"I've got you," Cai says, reaching into his backpack and handing Patrick the copy of Fin's Prophecy he and Phoebe were puzzling over yesterday afternoon when I got to Phoebe's house.

"Is this what you based your binding spell on?" Patrick asks me as he takes the paper from Cai.

"Binding spell?" Cai asks.

"So . . . I may have gone a bit rogue," I say. I explain my attempted binding spell to Cai and Phoebe while Patrick reads through Fin's Prophecy. "And obviously it didn't *work* work," I finish. "But I sort of—" I break off. I really don't want to tell Cai and Phoebe about my period. But the second I think that I see Cai's eyebrows rise. "Cai!"

"Sorry." He winces. "But you might as well tell us, and periods aren't embarrassing or anything."

"Oh, you're on your period too?" Phoebe asks. "I got mine a few days ago."

"This is kind of my first one," I explain. And I feel my cheeks reddening even though I know it's nothing to be embarrassed about. *Wouldn't mind if you took some of this particular emotion away*, I think loudly. And suddenly thinking about my period feels completely normal. Which it is. But it actually really feels that way. *Thanks*, I think. And Cai smiles.

"Anyway . . ." I say, drawing out the word as I recalibrate my thoughts. "Blood magic is sort of supercharged when a witch has their period—we call it the blood fairy."

"Oh, love that," Phoebe says. And I'm still mad at her, and at Cai. But that anger feels smaller today, especially when there's so much else to worry about. That thought brings my brain back to Patrick. Who's been quiet for a long time.

And when I look closer at him, I see tears in his eyes.

"Um, Patrick," I say, getting up from the couch and crossing over to him. "Are you okay?"

"This isn't a spell," he says. His voice is soft, but his words feel like a punch to my gut. "Or a prophecy," he adds.

"What do you mean?" I fight the urge to rip the paper out of his hands. How does he know? He wasn't there. He doesn't even know Fin.

"I know because I wrote it," he says. "Well, not the last part. I've never heard that before, but the first bit—" He breaks off and blinks a bunch of times, holding back the tears. "I know Orla hates me now, but that wasn't always the case. We loved each other once. I loved her in a way she couldn't love me back, but even after that." He pauses. "She was my best friend. And this was something I wrote for her, when I was trying to explain myself—trying to preserve our friendship."

"Then maybe I was meant to find you," I say. "Maybe Fin sent you to me."

"I don't know about all that," Patrick says. "But I wonder . . ." He pushes up from the chair and starts examining the bookshelves.

"How would Fin have known something you wrote to Ber's grandma a million years ago?" Phoebe asks.

"Your generation is overly prone to hyperbole," Patrick says as he continues to search.

"And your generation is overly prone to generational generalizations," Phoebe counters.

Great, just what I need, my friends bickering with Grandma Orla's nemesis slash . . . ex-boyfriend? This is getting too weird.

"Aha!" Patrick pulls a book from the shelf, turning back to us. He holds out a small leather-bound book I've never seen before.

"An owl," Cai says, looking up at me, eyes bright.

And there, on the cover of the little brown notebook, is an owl.

"May I?" Patrick asks. And I'm not sure whether I can give him permission or not. It's Grandma Orla's book. But Grandma Orla's gone, and Fin's clues were obviously leading us here, so I nod.

A sad smile splits Patrick's lined face as he runs a hand down the inside cover. And then he flips to the very back and starts to read.

"'My dearest Orla, I know you may have stopped reading this, that perhaps you've abandoned this entirely. Abandoned me entirely. I'm sorry I can't convince you of what I know in my heart is true. I'll leave you with this and hope you might find your way back to our friendship someday. The key is the story you tell yourself.'" As he reads, I hear the words of Fin's Prophecy. But he's right, it's not a prophecy at all. And it's not Fin's. It's Patrick's and Grandma Orla's. "'Questions asked together, spoken aloud, or held silently in our hearts keep us connected.'" But after he reads that line, he keeps going, reading something I've never heard before. Something that isn't part of what Fin left in Cai's mind. "'You are a mystery to me, Orla. Your magic is fierce and wild in a way that takes my breath away.'" Patrick breaks off, his cheeks going a bit pink. "I'm just going to stop there. But do you see?"

"Not really," Cai says.

"Ah, yes, well, I suppose I should explain that—" Patrick closes the notebook reverently and takes a deep breath. "I had this theory, which rather offended your grandmother."

"Which was?" Phoebe prompts at the same time Cai goes, "Whoa!"

"He can kind of read your mind," I explain when Patrick frowns.

"Not, like, *read* read," Cai says. "Okay, well, maybe sometimes—"

"What was the theory?" I ask, cutting off Cai's half-baked explanation for his creepily increasing mind magic.

Patrick taps the notebook with his middle finger, as if he's trying to decide how much to tell us.

"You might as well just say," I prompt. "Cai's already read your mind and will tell us."

"I mean . . ." Cai looks between Patrick and me, and it's kind of adorable how torn he looks. But I know he'd tell me. If Patrick doesn't. But he will.

"Well." Patrick takes a deep, dramatic breath. "I've always thought Orla, and several other witches of our generation, have been to the demon dimension before."

And it's official. My brain is broken. Because he can't have just said he thinks Grandma Orla, *my* Grandma Orla, has been to the demon dimension. Can he?

CHAPTER TWENTY-ONE

a (metaphorical) blizzard of confusion

"Like, before now?" I ask. Which feels like both the obvious question and completely bananas.

"It's a theory I developed in my youth," Patrick explains, sitting back down and settling the notebook on his lap. "That the way modern blood witches had interpreted the concept of balance was flawed."

"Fin *did* go on and on about the balance," Cai says, raising his eyebrows as if this all makes sense instead of being absolutely absurd.

"I'm still not hearing a theory here," I say, crossing my arms. I'm not sure why I'm defensive. I know Grandma Orla was—is—wrong about a lot. But there *are* good reasons for some of the things she taught us.

"I wanted to conjure Mysteries," Patrick says. "I

wanted to revisit questions in spells and extensions of narrative purpose."

"Like Maeve's idea," Cai whispers. "And your binding spell that Fin hijacked."

"No wonder Grandma Orla didn't reply to your letter," I say. But then another thought bashes all my other thoughts out of the way. "Wait, but is the end of Fin's—well, whatever it is—if those lines weren't from your letter, what were they from?"

"What were they again?" Patrick asks.

And I don't need to hand him the paper. I know them by heart.

"'Find your story—the thread only you can weave in the tapestry of magic. But it must be true. Only then will you find us. Only then will you bring her home.'"

Patrick frowns, looking off to the left. And I can practically see his mind working, trying to place the words. But he can't. And he shakes his head.

"I think those are just for you," he says. "What do you think they mean?"

And I want to scream at the question, because that's exactly what I've been trying to figure out for weeks.

Cai puts his hand on my shoulder, silently asking if I want him to take away this blizzard of confusion and anger and disappointment raging inside me. But I shake my head. I don't want to lose a single feeling about

Grandma Orla, not even the bad ones. Because then what if I give up like Mom did?

At that exact second, my phone buzzes in my pocket. Once. Twice. It's Mom's pattern.

"Shh!" I wave my hands, shushing everyone so I can answer. Even though they weren't actually talking. But it's Cai and Phoebe, they could start at any moment, and Patrick has proven pretty chatty too.

"Hey Mom," I say, trying to make my voice sound totally normal.

"Hey Ber, did Cai and Phoebe find you? I thought you might be in my mom's house again."

My throat tightens at "again." Does she know I've been coming in here looking for clues? I can't worry about that right now.

"Yeah, they found me. Everything okay?"

"It's just dinnertime, sweetie," she says. "They can join us if they want. I made a casserole big enough to feed an Abomination demon. And Clío is getting a bit restless without you."

"Oh, ummm." I'm not sure what to say. I can't exactly tell Mom that we can't come in to dinner, we're sorting through the messy mystery my messy Mystery demon left us with Grandma Orla's nemesis.

"If Cai's and Phoebe's parents say it's okay, you can hang out for a bit longer after dinner, but I need you to come in for dinner and need confirmation from their parents they can stay."

"Yeah, okay," I say. "We'll be in soon."

"*Soon* soon, Ber, as in the next five minutes. But three minutes would be better." She pauses and for a second, I think she's hung up, but then she says, "I wanted to give you some space today, you're going through a lot, but I haven't forgotten what you and Cai pulled at the Blood Moon gathering last week. Don't stretch the slack I'm giving you too far, okay?"

"Okay," I agree.

"Love you," Mom says. And then she does hang up.

"So . . . did you hear that?" I ask.

"Am I invited to dinner?" Patrick asks.

"Absolutely not," I say.

"I think we should stay," Cai says. "We can tell your parents we were just cheering you up and apologizing." He looks pointedly at Phoebe, who winces.

"Yeah, and then we'll get to the bottom of the rest of this . . ." Phoebe trails off. "Later?"

"Tonight," I say. "We need to do this tonight."

"Do what?" Cai asks.

"I'm not sure yet, but something," I say. "I can just feel it. Time passes differently in the demon dimension. We have to do something, and we have to do it tonight."

"Wouldn't it make more sense to wait for Samhain?"

Cai asks. "Just because the Veil is thinnest, and that's only a week away."

"A week could be a year in the demon dimension," I say.

"Or it could be a second," Phoebe says. I glare at her and she holds out her hands. "Sorry, just, like, in theory. But I agree, we need to do something, stat."

"We?" I ask. "You're going to help?"

"Obviously," she says.

"Well, good, but what are we going to do?" I ask. "We can't risk making another Tairseach, my binding spell didn't work—well, didn't work the way I intended. And now we know Grandma Orla and Fin are fighting and the Kalispell Coven is hurting the Mysteries and—well, I'm tired of theories and stories and I just want to fix this mess once and for all."

"I agree," Patrick says.

"Wait, really?" I ask. I'm so used to adults being the so-called voice of reason that I was fully prepared for him to march right into the house and give us up to Mom and Dad.

"I think if we're going to do anything, it would be best to try while you are still menstruating."

Even though Cai took away my weird squiggly feelings about my period, I still am not thrilled with Patrick's particular phrasing.

"Do you have to say it like that?" I mutter, but I don't actually want to argue with him while he's agreeing with me.

"I shall refrain from mentioning the blood fairy again," Patrick says, settling back into the chair and crossing one leg over the other. "You lads go have dinner and I'll be here searching for clues."

"You'll be here snooping through Grandma Orla's stuff?" I correct him.

"I mean, I could take those multiple Directs you mentioned and . . ."

"No!" Cai, Phoebe, and I all shout at the same time. Even Mars meows a protest.

"Well, it's been at least the three minutes your mother mentioned," Patrick says. "Go on."

"And you'll be here when we get back?" I ask.

"That's the intention," Patrick says. And I think that's the best I'm going to get for now. I scoop up Mars and follow Phoebe and Cai back out of the house.

As Cai races across the yard with Frangi, Phoebe taps my arm.

"Ber, I'm really sorry about yesterday," she says.

"Oh, yeah." I get ready to shrug and say it's fine, but I don't. I just wait to hear what else she's going to say.

"I didn't understand," she says. "And I thought I did, and that can be worse than not understanding at all, you know?"

I pause and really think about that for a second. Because I agree. It's kind of the same as when I thought I knew about other magics, but I didn't know anything at all. And I still feel like I don't.

"Yeah," I say. "I do. Thank you for apologizing."

"I really felt terrible," she says as we keep walking across the yard. "I don't know any other type one diabetics. It sounds really scary."

"It is," I say. "But it's almost more frustrating than scary? It's hard to explain."

"Whatever you're up for sharing with me, I want to understand," Phoebe says. "Really."

"Thanks," I say, just as we get to the porch. Cai's already inside, chatting away with my parents like nothing is wrong. Cool as a cucumber. Heck, he's probably putting their minds at ease. Which freaks me out a little. I don't want him manipulating them, but I can't pretend it isn't useful.

"Phoebe! Great to see you!" Dad puts out his arms and Phoebe gives him a hug.

Mom raises her eyebrows, and I can tell she's asking if I'm okay. Asking about the blood fairy. Asking about what she told me about not being able to get Grandma Orla back. Mom does that, asks a bunch of questions with just her eyebrows. It's impressive. I try to make my smile answer enough for all of them.

I help carry the glasses to the table and settle down in

my usual seat. Maeve's not here, so Cai takes her chair, and Dad grabs an extra chair for Phoebe as Clío curls up at my feet. Grandma Orla's chair is empty at the head of the table. And I'm glad Dad didn't offer it to Phoebe instead. But how soon will Mom start letting people sit there if we don't get her back?

I just want things to go back to normal.

Well, not normal. Not the way they were before. Some things are better now, even without Grandma Orla here.

And the thought makes me go cold all over. Because it feels like what Maeve was saying. About it being easier to date Tempest without Grandma Orla here.

But then I think about Patrick Walsh out in Grandma Orla's house. I think about the letter he wrote her, how Grandma Orla had a whole life before I even existed. How maybe I don't know her that well at all. Patrick tried to get her to listen about Mysteries years and years ago and she wouldn't.

But that's just more reason for us to get to her, and as soon as possible.

And we don't give up on people just because they are wrong about something. At least I don't.

CHAPTER TWENTY-TWO
the thread only i can weave

"Ber, could I talk with you for a second?" Mom asks. "Alone."

We just finished dinner, and I thought I was going to be able to sneak away without Mom cornering me with whatever had been dragging her eyes back to me every two minutes the whole meal. I guess not. Hopefully it's just about the blood fairy. I bet she doesn't want to bring it up in front of Cai.

"Oh yeah, sure," I say. "But Cai and Phoebe and I can still hang out for a bit after, right?"

I cross my fingers behind my back, hoping I'm not being too desperate. Just a normal amount of desperate. The perfect level of desperation that activates parent guilt and chronically-ill-kid pity.

"Maybe," Mom says. "Can you two wait down here while I talk with Ber for a minute?"

"Sure!" Phoebe says brightly, and plops down onto the couch where Clío, Mars, and Frangi all pile on top of her. Cai's too busy chatting with Dad to even notice. Or that's what I think until he turns and smiles and waves. And I wonder if he's responding to what my mom said or what I was thinking.

I follow Mom upstairs, ready to tell her I'm actually feeling much better, and maybe the blood fairy isn't so bad after all. And my blood sugar is even stable. But as I follow her into my room, I freeze.

The partially burned candle, discarded spell draft, and my lancet thingy are all sitting on my bedside table when I definitely hid them in the drawer specifically to avoid this exact scenario. I'm absolutely positive my guilt is written all over my face as Mom crosses her arms and tilts her head to the side. Waiting.

Of course, the first thing that blurts out of my mouth is "What were you doing snooping in my room?" Great, off to a good start here.

"I was getting your duvet to wash," Mom says. Right. The bloody duvet. From the bloody blood fairy.

"Oh, right" is all I can think to say.

"Well? What were you doing, Ber? Did you try to conjure alone?"

"No," I say quickly. Hopefully not too quickly. "I just—" I don't have to fake the fear and sadness in my voice, because whatever I say next could ruin everything. "I just wanted to feel closer to her. And I was hoping I might convince you—but that was before . . ." I trail off and Mom's face falls.

"Before what we talked about in the bathroom?" she asks.

I nod as tears fill my eyes. And they are angry tears. Because I'm furious that she said those things, that she clearly still thinks there's no chance. I wish I could trust her, could tell her about Patrick and get her to help us. But I know I can't. I know I have to lie.

"I know you're right," I say. I hate this. I hate this so much. Because she's not right. But if I can convince her she is, that I've seen her point, that I'm giving up on Grandma Orla too, maybe she'll leave me alone long enough to actually rescue her. "I don't want to believe it, 'cuz it hurts too much, you know?"

Mom crosses to me in a single stride and pulls me to her. I feel like a traitor. To her and to Grandma Orla. But I keep going.

"She might be gone, and I'm not ready to give up on that. So, I just . . . wanted to feel closer to her. And I'll try, I'm trying . . . to accept—" I break off. I can't say it. But thankfully I don't have to. Mom thinks I'm too upset and she just hugs me closer. She's right. I am too upset. But not at Grandma Orla or even the world. At her.

"So can I hang out with my friends for a little while longer?" I ask, finally pulling back from her hug and wiping away tears. She's crying too and I remind myself that is absolutely not my fault.

"Yeah, Ber, of course," Mom says. "But I don't want you guys out in Grandma Orla's house after eight, okay?"

I pull my phone out and see that it's 7:37. Which absolutely is not enough time, but I'll burn that bridge when I come to it, as Grandma Orla says.

"Thanks," I say instead. "I love you," I add, even though I'm not entirely sure I mean it in that moment. But it does the trick, and Mom kisses the top of my head before I run downstairs and collect my friends and race back to Grandma Orla's house.

"Okay, so technically we have . . ." I glance at my phone again. 7:41. "Nineteen minutes until we're supposed to be back inside."

"Yeah, my grandma's coming to get me at eight fifteen too," Phoebe says.

"Well, I hope you figured it all out while we were having dinner," I say to Patrick as we waltz into Grandma Orla's study to find him . . . asleep. Just absolutely zonked. Stretched out on the couch. Head drooped down to his chest and snoring while Nimby purrs on his lap.

"Or not," Cai says as Patrick grumbles himself awake. There's a mostly full cup of tea and a mostly empty roll of the flavors of Hobnobs you can only get in Ireland. I almost feel bad for how angry Grandma Orla is going to be at him when she finds out he ate the cookies she'd been saving for almost a year.

"Well, I guess you don't need the piece of pie I snuck out for you," I say, setting it on the bookcase, out of range of Clío, who is giving me her most pathetic *I need pie* doggy stare.

"Well, I wouldn't exactly say that," Patrick says, pushing himself up and holding out his hand for the plate.

"We don't have time for pie, we need a plan," Phoebe says.

"I think pie is the perfect accompaniment to planning," Patrick says, digging right in.

"Maybe we should wait for another night," Cai says.

"Absolutely not," I say. "I can just feel it, it has to be now."

"Yeah, okay, but *how*?" Phoebe says. "If the first part of the not-prophecy is *not* a spell, what was it?"

"A reminder," I say. And suddenly, I feel like Maeve. The ideas clicking into place faster than I can process them. And it's like I'm chasing after my own mind, worried it might leave me behind.

"Cai, a little help here?" I ask, and it takes him a second to catch on, but I open my mind to him completely and hope he can catch the pieces I miss as I try to put together the puzzle that's been forming in the back of my brain for weeks. And I think lying to my mom just gave me the corner piece that everything is anchored to.

"The spell needs to be about Grandma Orla," I say. "The thread only *I* can weave in the tapestry of magic. Only then will I find *her*. Only then will I bring *her* home. I was focusing on Fin because I'd bound them before, and they're a demon and can travel between dimensions. But you think people have gone to the demon dimension before, right?"

I turn to Patrick, who is mid-chomp on a huge bite of pie.

"I do," he says through the crumbly bite. He chews a few times and swigs down the remainder of his tea before he continues. "I think blood witches used to travel between the dimensions regularly, in fact. And I think your grandmother was one of those witches."

"So maybe it's in my blood," I say. "Maybe I'm meant to go to the demon dimension. Maybe that's the key too. That it's about going and bringing her home, not just pulling her back through the Veil."

"What was that you were just thinking about the

'tapestry of magic'?" Cai asks, taking my hand. "Think about that again."

I try, but I don't think I was even aware of the thought.

"It's gone," I say. "Why? What was I thinking?"

"Wait, are you, like, helping her sort through her thoughts?" Phoebe asks.

"Kinda," Cai says. "I'm trying." He squeezes my hand. "Ber, there's something about the tapestry of magic bit of Fin's message that we're missing, and I think you were almost there. Something about your grandma going to the demon dimension, and memories, and . . ." He trails off, scrunching up his face in concentration.

"Okay, wait," I say. "The first bits of Fin's prophecy or message or whatever, they may have been Patrick's letter to Grandma Orla, but that doesn't mean they aren't important."

"Good call," Cai says. "Maybe the plant imagery Phoebe and I were looking into yesterday is actually important."

"Oh, that was just my attempt at poetry," Patrick says, polishing off the last of the pie and setting the plate on the floor for the cats and Clío. She looks at me first and only joins in licking it clean once I nod.

"I was really interested in plant magic at the time,"

Patrick continues. "I was researching—and dabbling in—many magics at the time, which Orla and Bernadette were horrified by."

"You knew my great-great-grandma?" I ask.

"Not well," Patrick says. "Your coven had already moved across the Atlantic and I only met Orla when I was studying in New York."

"Wait, you studied plant magic?" Phoebe asks. "What kind of plant magic?"

"I'm not entirely sure," Patrick says. "I was convinced certain plants in Ireland were not only not native to Ireland, but from another dimension. It was something of an obsession, but I was never able to prove my hypothesis, and I got rather obsessed with weather magic soon after. I had a much greater propensity for it and it's a bit easier to be obsessed with the things you're naturally good at, I find."

And that phrase, *naturally good at*, lights something up in my brain.

"You're naturally good at pulling things through the Veil," Cai says to me. "In fact, your blood is so good at it, you do it on accident."

"Oh dear," Patrick says. "Because of the blood testing, for the diabetes?"

I nod, waving a hand at him, because I have to follow this thought through without getting distracted. We're running out of time.

"What if I don't need a spell," I think aloud. "What if it's simpler than that. What if—" But the idea dissolves like a drop of blood in a pool of water. "Dangit, I was so close, I could feel it."

"Ber." Phoebe's voice cuts through my thoughts and I want to scream at her. Which is fully an overreaction, but I'm fully freaking out.

"Sorry, Ber, but—the tapestry of magic," Phoebe says. "What if it's a real tapestry? The first part of Fin's message was an actual letter written in this actual journal. So what if . . . I don't know. Could there be a map to the demon dimension or something?"

"That doesn't make any sense." My voice is harsher than I mean it to be, but Phoebe doesn't seem fazed. "The thread only I can weave in the tapestry of magic," I correct her. "It's a metaphor. Fin loves metaphors too much for this to be about a literal tapestry. I can't even sew or anything."

"Oh!" Cai's eyes go wide, and he starts bouncing on his toes. "Oh, oh, oh. What if—what if—"

"Spit it out, Cai!" Phoebe groans.

"Okay, but what if it was all intentional, the whole message, I mean. But it wasn't *logical*." He looks between us like this explains everything, but when we stare blankly back, he keeps talking. "Fin isn't haphazard, but their mind also doesn't work like ours. I think I need to think like a Mystery."

"Can you do that?" I ask.

"I can try," Cai says.

"Then try!" Phoebe says, putting her hands on her hips and giving Cai an almost hilarious *why didn't you think of this weeks ago* look that I low-key appreciate.

"We need things that hold meaning and history and stories," Cai says. His eyes are closed and his voice is soft, and I can't help but hear the uncertainty in it. "Something of yours, something of Orla's, and . . ." He trails off and his nose scrunches up. "Something of a Mystery?"

"Is that a question?" Phoebe asks.

"I don't know, I'm doing my best here," Cai snaps. Cai. Snaps. As in Cai shows outward annoyance. Okay, he's really stressed about this.

"Something you're super attached to," Cai says.

"But if we're thinking like Fin, that has to be my pump, right?" I'm joking, but Cai's eyes pop open.

"Okay, that actually could work," he says.

"Work how? I'm not messing with my insulin pump," I say. "I was fully kidding."

"And Fin is fully the kidding-est kidder in the history of . . . well, anything," Cai says.

"Well, we're in your grandma's house, so finding something of hers should be easy," Phoebe says.

Mars and Frangi pick that moment to jump up on the couch and start yowling.

"I know, I know, we're almost out of time," I say. My pump says it's only three minutes to eight.

"The blanket!" Cai says. "They're saying Grandma Orla is super attached to this blanket. Well, I'm not sure super attached is the right cat translation, but—"

"It was her baby blanket," I say.

"Perfect," Cai says. "Great job," he adds to Frangi and Mars, who both start purring furiously.

"What else do we need?" I ask. "What did you mean by 'something of a Mystery'?"

"I don't know," Cai says with a groan. "It just felt right."

"A story," Patrick says. "Your story. Orla ran from hers, she's a secretive woman who wants to control the narrative. From a family of witches who have controlled many of the stories that form our culture as blood witches. You need to tell your story, Bernadette."

"The story is the spell," Cai says, nodding. "And you're also going to need blood," he adds.

"Well, obviously," Patrick says. "She's a blood witch, a Crowley, and a diabetic. And she's having her first visit from the blood fairy. Her story wouldn't be even remotely true without blood."

"And what we all need is more time," Cai says. "I'll be right back."

And before I can stop him, or even think to stop him, Cai kisses me on the cheek and runs back through Grandma Orla's house and out the front door.

CHAPTER TWENTY-THREE
blood is easy, the truth is harder

"Blood is easy, the truth is harder," Patrick says as the door of Grandma Orla's house slams behind Cai. I cross to the far side of the room and peek through the curtains to see Cai run across the yard, bound up the porch steps, and rush into the main house.

"What do you mean?" I ask, turning back to Patrick after pulling the curtains shut again.

"Truth is complicated," Patrick says. "Blood is complicated too, but it's also straightforward. The sacrifice that parts the Veil. A drop of blood. You were taught that spells are declarations, yes?"

I nod.

"And require certainty of mind," he continues.

"Yeah, that part has been a bit of a struggle for me,"

I say. Clío bumps her head into my knee, and I reach out a hand for her to alert, but she just nuzzles into it and I drop onto the floor and let her drape herself over my lap.

"It was hard for me too," Patrick says. "When I was your age especially, but even now."

"Really?" I ask.

"Oh, yes." He smiles and settles back onto the couch, where Nimby immediately pounces on his lap. "But I've learned something important in my seventy-four years in this dimension," he says. "Which is that uncertainty has power too. As you saw when you bound your Mystery demon."

"My question, you mean?"

"And your life," Patrick says. "Certainty is great for retaining control, and when you're conjuring demons, it's a pretty good idea to focus on control." He laughs. "I'm not saying I disagree with all the Crowley philosophies. I'm not quite the anarchist your grandmother thinks I am."

"But why are you helping us?" I ask. "Why are you helping me?"

"Well, we've not yet fully established I am," Patrick says. "But you remind me a lot of her. Of Orla, when she was not much older than you. And I guess I still love her, even after all these years."

"Um, you know she's a lesbian, right?" The question feels a bit rude but also kinda important. I don't want this old guy chasing after my grandma through the demon dimension hoping for some romantic happily ever after.

Patrick barks out a laugh that shakes his whole body and startles Nimby from his lap.

"Oh, I think I might have been the first person to learn that fact and I have not forgotten it," he says. "Don't worry. I'm not some poor lovesick schoolboy. At least not about Orla."

I decide to completely ignore the last part of that statement for my general mental well-being. Which is already hanging by a thread.

"If we make it back, will you tell me what she was like?" I ask. "You know, if she doesn't kill us for rescuing her."

"I'm certain she will claim that no rescue was necessary," Patrick says. "But yes, I'd love to tell you about Orla and my youth. If I can remember it. Your past gets slipperier and slipperier the further you get from it, I find."

"Agreed," Phoebe adds emphatically. As if she isn't twelve.

But Patrick just smiles at her and I hear the front door of Grandma Orla's house open and close again. A second later, Cai rushes into the room.

"So, we've got some extra time now," he says. "And your parents decided to go to bed super early."

"Decided?" I ask, my heart squeezing in my chest. I don't love the idea of Cai mind-magicking my parents. But I do have to admit I like the idea of them interrupting our spell even less.

Cai shrugs and winces. I decide to deal with that whole situation later. A tiny part of my brain gets really pokey, trying to bring my attention to just how many things I'm shoving away for later, but I tell it to pipe down.

"My grandma is still probably going to show up in ten minutes," Phoebe says.

"Maybe we should just wait until after—" Cai starts, but Phoebe cuts him off.

"Oh, no way you're going and exploring another dimension without me. Plus, you needed me last time. There's no way you could have stopped the Kalispell Coven without me. Not an option. I'm coming."

"Actually, I'm not sure—" Patrick starts, but Phoebe cuts him off too.

"You think blood witches are stubborn, you should try plant mages," she says, staring Patrick down until he shrugs. "Okay then, let's get started. What do we need to do? How can we help?"

We all look to Cai, and then Patrick, and then everyone stares at me.

And in that moment, I miss Grandma Orla so much I feel like I might just collapse into a useless pile of goo. She would know what to do.

"You will know what to do," Cai says, taking my hand. "And missing her is good. Missing her is the point. Let's go find her."

"Okay," I say, taking a deep breath. "My pump, her baby blanket, some blood, and our story?"

"Your story," Cai corrects me. "Your truth."

"The thread only I can weave in the tapestry of magic," I repeat to myself.

"I do think the actual passage through the Veil will require blood from each of us," Patrick says. "Which is why perhaps you two should remain in this dimension."

Cai and Phoebe immediately disagree, and I let them argue it out with Patrick as I try to figure out what the heck my truth is. Patrick's right, blood is simpler. I can stab my finger, and blood will come out. If it doesn't, I just stab again until it does. But I'm not sure where to metaphorically stab myself for the truth.

"You know yourself better than most people our age," Cai says, startling me out of my thoughts by crashing into them. "Trust yourself," he adds. "I trust you."

"Will you help me?" I ask.

"Of course," he says. "But not in the way you're asking. I will support you; I will go to the demon dimension with you *when* this works, but you don't need my help to tell your story."

"Um, maybe we should go outside though?" Phoebe chimes in. "Just, you know, with the whole interdimensional travel thing. In case anything else comes through?"

"Grandma's garden," I say. "It's on the back side of the house. It's small, and we need to be careful not to trample anything."

"Duh!" Phoebe says. "Let's go. We've got five minutes before *my* grandma shows up, and she's never late."

"Fact," Cai says as he scoops up Frangi and Mars.

"Clío, you should stay here," I say.

But Cai shakes his head. "She wants to come," he says. "You need her."

And he's right. She may be the newest member of my family, but she's family. I can't leave her behind. That wouldn't be my truth.

I grab Grandma Orla's blanket and lead everyone down the hall and out the back door. Grandma Orla's garden is super small. It has high walls that are covered with vines, and the leaves are all bright reds and burnt orange this late in the fall. It's dark, but the light from a neighbor's backyard filters into the yard just a bit, casting an eerie orange-yellow glow. We stick to the small path, all bunched together until Phoebe can direct us to places to stand that won't hurt any of the plants.

I hook Grandma Orla's blanket over one arm as I take my pump in one hand and my lancet in the other.

"Wait, how are you going to prick your fingers?" I ask Cai and Phoebe as Patrick pulls his dagger from under his sweater.

"I'll use a thorn from one of the roses," Phoebe says. "Do you want one, Cai?"

Cai shakes his head and fumbles with his jacket. "I've got my pride pin," he says.

"Clío, this may get scary, but you're going to get to meet Grandma Orla soon, so it'll be worth it, okay?" I look down at my dog, whose tail wags furiously, and I'm not sure if I should ask Cai to warn her about what's coming, or just be glad she's up for anything. As long as she's with me.

Mars, Frangi, and Nimby sit next to her, their own tails swishing slowly across the dirt, their eyes glowing in the darkness.

"Just tell your story," Patrick says. "And we'll follow your lead."

I wish I could invite Cai into my head to take away my self-doubt, but that's part of me too, I guess. So I start to tell my story.

"My name is Bernadette Orla Baron Crowley," I say. "I'm a blood witch and a diabetic." Huh, I hadn't realized how big a part of me diabetes was already. But it feels both sad and powerful to claim it, so I keep going. "I'm trying to understand my place in the tapestry of magic, but I don't think I do yet. And I'm not sure I can without my grandma, Orla Crowley. I love her with my entire heart, and probably some other organs too." Cai laughs quietly, and I'm worried I've messed up, because this isn't a joke. This is so serious. But there's silly stuff in the serious moments too. And Grandma Orla knows that better than most people. "I don't know who I am without her," I say, and I can feel my throat going tight, but I keep talking. "And I'm not ready to find out. I'm asking for a chance to change and grow with her." My skin starts to tingle and the hairs on the back of my neck stand on end. "I'm asking questions. And I want to keep asking questions. And I'm—" I swallow. This last bit feels different. But I remember what Cai said and I try to trust myself.

I get my lancet ready, and I watch Cai, Phoebe, and Patrick get ready to pierce their own fingers. And then I say what I hope are the magic words.

"I'm the real Bernadette Crowley, and Finley MacIntire taught me I'm brave and strong and out of control. They have profound and—" I pause, trying to remember the exact word Fin used, and then I find it. "They have profound and irrevocable faith in my power, and so do I."

And then we prick our fingers and hold our breath. And then, after a moment and forever, and also all at once, the garden starts to glow.

PART THREE

Forgotten Answers

CHAPTER TWENTY-FOUR
all things unsubstantiated

It takes me a moment to realize the garden isn't glowing, I am. And so is Patrick. Before I can see if my friends or the animals are, I hear shouts.

"Ber? Cai? Phoebe?"

It's Mom. And then Dad chimes in too.

No, we are so close. The spell is working. What did I do wrong? Why are we still in this dimension? And why are we glowing?

But then I hear my name again. Softer. Lilting. Questioning.

"Is that you, Little Bernadette?"

"Fin!" I shout, just as I see my parents come into the garden.

And then I feel Fin's hand in mine, their soft, sleek fur.

I'm vaguely aware of Patrick letting out a small "oh" and then there's a whooshing sensation. It's almost like traveling by Direct demon, but instead of the pull coming from my middle toward something, it's like my entire body is being pulled in every direction all at once. If it weren't so weird it would be the best stretch ever. And my parents are fading from sight, and a whole new landscape comes into view.

The ground feels strange. Almost like a trampoline. Bouncy but also firm. At first glance, our surroundings don't look that different from the forest around Missoula. Maybe just a bit more lush. But as I continue to look, the shapes and colors are different. Light seems to come from . . . everywhere? And the harder I look, the more I try to get my eyes to focus, the more things seem to shift and change. It's almost dizzying. But it doesn't actually make me dizzy.

"It worked," I whisper. "The story worked. The spell worked!" I feel like jumping up and down, but I'm slightly worried I might bounce away on the springy ground.

"Indeed, it did," Fin says. "Though you actually only needed about seven of those words."

"Which seven?" I ask.

"Well, where would be the fun in telling you that?" And it's Fin. Trickster, infuriating, riddle-riddled Fin. I have them back. Well, they have me back? But then the reality of what we just did sinks all the way in. And I fully panic. Because this is not Earth. This is another dimension. What was I thinking? I'm a diabetic. Is there even insulin in the demon dimension?

"Oh no," I whisper. "Oh no, oh no, oh no." My whispers are now more like squeaks, and I can't stop.

"Bernadette, please, look at me." Fin's voice barely breaks through the screaming in my mind. What have I done?

Clío puts her paws on my thigh, takes the edge of my sweater in her jaws, and nearly tugs me over. I automatically put out my hand for her to alert, but she doesn't. She just sits, doggy eyebrows tilted in concern, and whines.

"What is it?" I ask, sinking down to a crouch and looking into her face.

"Ah, I see," Fin says. "She's a being without a purpose."

I'm in another dimension. Reality is crashing back in, and my chest and throat go all tight and I feel like I *should* be crying. My eyes burn, but the tears don't fall. Actually, the tears just . . . don't exist? What is going on?

I turn to Fin and their wolfish face wears a sly grin.

"Things work differently here. You will not require insulin, or food, or sleep. And your canine companion here is quite confused, as technically, I believe you don't have any blood sugar. At least not in the way you do in your home dimension."

I stare at them, not understanding a single word

they're saying. Maybe I don't have brain cells here either. At least not functioning ones.

"You're going to be okay," Fin says, with more patience in their voice than I've ever heard. "Think of this dimension as a kind of . . . suspended animation. Here, we just exist. Nothing needs to be created or destroyed, there is no entropy, no laws of physics that a human might recognize. Not that your kind has yet truly understood your own dimension thoroughly and exhaustibly, but even so—"

"Got it," I say. Even though I don't. But I know from experience that I shouldn't let Fin get momentum if they're headed for any kind of pseudo-scientific lecture type situation. "I don't need insulin here? That's what you're saying?" I look down at my pump, wondering whether I should turn it off. But as I push the buttons on the screen, a swirling spiral of white pixels glows up at me.

"I'd keep track of that strange little box, as you'll need it when you return to your dimension," Fin explains. "But for now, it will not function, and you will remain alive. Well, not technically alive, but—"

"Fin!"

"Technicalities, yes. But Bernadette!" Their eyes narrow and they shake their head.

"You followed my clues, you brilliant witch. I knew you would. Please, tell me. How long did it take? How much time has passed in your dimension? You look relatively the same, though you've clearly added a canine to your coven. Odd choice, but I approve."

And at the word *coven* my heart clenches. But then I hear a voice. The best voice in the entire world.

"Bernie!" Grandma Orla shouts. She's running through the strange trees, a distinct bounce to her step. Her sleek gray cat Dar right beside her. I rush to her and when we meet, we smash together so hard it almost hurts. But I don't care.

"I missed you so much," I say into Grandma Orla's sweater. And she's real. She's her perfect, soft, grandma-shaped self. And it's like the hole in my chest is filled and then some.

"I missed you too, my dear girl," she says, stroking my hair. "My brilliant, brave Bernie. And who's this?" She looks down at Clío, who's bumping into Grandma Orla's leg with her head.

"This is Clío, my diabetes dog," I explain, laughing as my dog smiles up at us. "It's short for Clíodhna. Like from the stories you told me."

"Not just stories," Fin says. "Though most legends are always more than they seem."

"Oh, Bernie," Grandma Orla says, pulling me to her again. Dar yowls, and I wonder if it's a yowl of hello or protest at the newest member of the family being a dog. But I don't look down to check. Because Grandma Orla's hugging me. And it's the best feeling in the entire world. I just stay there, hugging my grandma, for a long time. My throat is tight and my heart aches, but in a good way. I found her. We found her. But as I slowly release my grandma and look around, really look around, I don't see Cai and Phoebe anywhere.

"Where are Cai and Phoebe?" I ask.

"Only blood witches and their familiars can venture into the demon dimension." Grandma Orla's voice is low, and I turn to see she's not actually looking at me, she's looking at Patrick.

Oh. Right. I fully brought Grandma Orla's nemesis on her rescue mission. And left my friends behind.

"Orla," Patrick says. "It's been . . . well, it's been a long time, hasn't it?"

"Not long enough," Grandma Orla mutters.

"Grandma, please," I say, grabbing her hand. "I was trying to get you back and I lit the candle you gave me and tried to bind another Mystery, but Patrick showed up instead."

"Your powerful granddaughter here fully commandeered a Direct I was taking to my grandson Dara's," Patrick says. "Unsettling, but I can't deny it was a thrill."

"Bernie, you did what?" Grandma stares between me and Patrick as Fin smirks, clearly delighted by this rather uncomfortable double reunion.

"I had to find you," I say, squeezing Grandma Orla's

hand harder. "I was trying to bring you home, but then we realized you might need me here. Need us here. And Patrick—" I break off as Grandma Orla turns to Patrick, fierceness written on every line of her face.

"You helped my Bernie?" she asks.

"I did," Patrick says. "And I was only ever trying to help you, Orla. All those years ago."

Grandma Orla pulls her hand from mine and stoops, scooping Dar up onto her shoulder. I'm pretty sure she's also taking the opportunity to look away as she tries to process all of this. Grandma Orla always gets self-conscious about seeming confused. Certainty of mind is her default setting and the only one she ever wants anyone to see. And now that I think about it, I think that's what got us into this whole mess in the first place.

"Where is the Kalispell Coven?" I ask Fin, looking around the clearing and wondering if a dozen rogue witches are about to come barreling down on us.

"Last I heard, Chaos Canyon," Fin says.

"Last you heard? What have you been doing here?"

"Well, that's rather hard to say, as time doesn't precisely exist and—"

"We've been getting some things straight," Grandma Orla says. "And catching up."

"Catching up?" I look between them, my mind

racing a million miles a minute. "I thought you were supposed to be catching *them*. You know, the rogue coven that disappeared into this dimension?"

"Well, you see, when time doesn't exist, urgency is rather less . . . urgent." Fin shrugs.

"We can revisit the whole 'time doesn't exist' thing later," I say.

"Technically later also doesn't exist," Fin starts, but I ignore them.

"We're here to help," I say. "I thought you needed our help." And there's this strange sensation in my chest that almost feels like disappointment. Which is absurd, because we did it. We traveled to another dimension. But then a horrible thought pops into my head, expanding like a Balloon demon until it escapes from my mouth. "Do you not want to come home?"

"Oh, no, Bernie, no," Grandma Orla says. She rushes to me, pulling me into a hug. "Things are just confusing here; you can never be certain how much time is passing in the mortal dimension. I very much wanted—want—to come home. To you and our whole family. There's just something I need to do first, something I need to understand."

"What?" I ask.

"You were right," Grandma Orla says. And it takes me a second to realize she's looking past me, at Patrick.

"Um, are you sure you're my grandma?" The words are out of my mouth before I can even think.

"I can confirm this is indeed Orla Crowley," Fin says. "The same Orla Crowley I knew as a child."

"Wait, what?" I stare between the two of them, waiting for a very necessary explanation, when I hear a mew high above me and to my left. A mew I recognize immediately.

"Mars?" I stare up into the trees. Or treelike plants. If they're plants at all. I hadn't realized Mars came into this dimension with us. And where is he now? He mews again. I try to move toward the sound, but the second I do, it seems to come from somewhere else. I move. The sound moves. "Mars!?"

"I'll get him," Fin says. "Mars, please do stay still for a moment, won't you?" they add. When I look over to them, they're climbing up one of the trees. Or the thing that looks like a tree. As Fin climbs, their hands sink into the bark of the trunk. Their pearly white feet disappear into the blue-green leaves as Clío presses into my legs.

As I bend down to give her head a reassuring pat, I hear a mew from so high above me it's almost imperceptible.

"Mars, please, the branches are just going to bring you higher and higher if you don't—"

I can't make out the end of Fin's sentence, but I think I hear a satisfied grunt. And then they plummet to the ground, Mars clutched in their arms. Fin hands me my cat, and I want to scold him, but he's shaking. Instead, I clutch him to my chest, kissing his little furry head.

"It's best if we all stay together," Fin says. "You may have noticed that matter here is a bit . . ."

"Squishy?" I finish. It seems silly but somehow the most accurate word I can find. For starters, the ground is squishy. Literally. But everything seems hard to pin down in a more metaphorical sense too. It's doing a number on my senses.

"I was going to say 'unsubstantiated,'" Fin says.

"Do you mean insubstantial?" Grandma Orla asks.

"No, I do not. I meant and continue to mean unsubstantiated."

"Doesn't that mean 'unproven'?" I can feel myself frowning and annoyance rises in my chest. I'd kind of blocked out this part of Fin's personality when I was thinking about our reunion.

"Indeed," Fin says. I can't believe they agree with me. Very out of character. "Much of my dimension is unproven."

And I want to laugh with relief and scream in frustration, which feels very much like a proper reunion with this particular Mystery demon. But then my brain rewinds to the bombshell Fin dropped before Mars started being carried away by trees.

"What do you mean you knew Grandma Orla as a kid?" I demand.

In response, Fin shushes me.

"Fin, seriously, I—" I protest, but they put a furry hand over my mouth, their eyes wide and worried. And that's when I hear the wings.

CHAPTER TWENTY-FIVE
the actual literal worst

"Bernadette, I need you to listen carefully, and do exactly as I say," Fin whispers.

I nod, ice sliding down my spine at the fear in their voice.

"I'm going to make you invisible," they say. "But that illusion will be broken immediately if you don't stay still. So, I'm going to need you to stay very, very still. Don't even breathe. You don't need to in this dimension anyway. Understand?"

I don't, but I nod, and then stop nodding and blink twice for yes. Even though we haven't established that code. Hopefully Fin understands. They hoist Clío higher on their shoulder and reach out their hand, muttering words in a language I don't understand as I stand very, very still and try not to breathe.

The not breathing thing is surprisingly easy when your lungs don't need oxygen, apparently. But the staying still thing is a whole different ball game. Especially when the demons whose wings I heard land. They drop to the ground right between Fin and Grandma Orla.

The one closest to Fin looks like a human woman, but with wings. And more beautiful and terrifying than any human woman I've ever seen. Also somehow just . . . wrong? Their waist and limbs are too long, their hair falls all the way to their feet, draping their body in a way that's almost cloth-like.

The other is basically a dragon. At least that's the category my brain wants to put it in. *Them* in, I correct myself. Because I'm fairly certain this is another Mystery.

The Mystery has red, shining skin that looks wet and two sets of translucent wings that are fully extended. They are at least a head taller than Fin, and I try to process their shining black claws and golden fangs, but then, as I start to count the fangs, I notice they have too many eyes. Not to be judgy or anything. There are just . . . a lot of eyes. Five of them. On three separate heads. And a socket that looks like it used to hold a sixth. Their wings fold against their back as they level their gazes at Grandma Orla.

"Cadwalader," Fin says, inclining their head toward the dragon-looking Mystery and taking a small, subtle step between me and the Mystery.

"Finley," the demon says. Their voices are musical and harsh at the same time. All three heads speak in unison, but not on the same pitch. And the result is super creepy, but also kind of weirdly beautiful.

"Witches," the other Mystery says, and her screeching voice makes me want to clap my hands over my ears. But I don't. Stay still. I have to stay still.

"Mysteries," Patrick Walsh says. His voice is filled with awe. And he's smiling. Maybe he's completely lost his mind. But maybe I have too. Maybe human logic and reasoning can't function in this dimension. Which would explain a lot about Fin, actually.

"Well, well, well," the humanlike Mystery screeches. "Cadwalader, you were right. Finley's witches are as strange as you said."

Finley's witches? I wonder. Trying not to blink. Or breathe. Or move.

"They're rather larger than I remembered though," Cadwalader says. The strange unison speak-singing of Cadwalader's three heads is unnerving and hard to follow. "I like this one," they say, leaning closer to Grandma Orla, who glares up at them one head at a time.

"I'm not sure that feeling is entirely mutual," Grandma Orla says, crossing her arms over her chest.

"Oh, yes," Cadwalader says. "This one is much more fun than the others back at Chaos Canyon. And she's got a cat and—oh!" All three of their heads tilt to the side in unison. "Oh, she's been here before. Oh, yes. I pick this one." And then they flap their wings twice and rise up into the air, carrying Grandma Orla and Dar with them.

"Put me down," she shouts. "How dare you?"

"Yes, I prefer the quiet ones anyway," the other Mystery screeches, before scooping up Patrick in their arms and taking off. Unlike Grandma Orla, Patrick seems delighted by this turn of events.

And I expect Fin to do something. I expect them to put a stop to this. They're not just going to let these demons fly off with Grandma Orla and Patrick, are they?

Except that's exactly what they do. And by the time I've run to where Grandma Orla was standing only a few seconds ago, they demons have disappeared into the pale lavender sky.

"What the heck, Fin?" I scream, rounding on the demon who I thought was my friend. "You just let them take them away?"

"I could only provide invisibility strong enough for three of you on such short notice," they say. "So I chose the canine, the cat, and yourself."

"But you let them take Grandma Orla away!"

"And how would you have suggested I stop them?"

Fin puts their hands on their—well, not hips, but where hips would be if they were a person—and stares me down.

"I'm not a Mystery demon!" I cry. "I don't know how things work here."

"Precisely," Fin says. "You do not know how things work here." There's an edge to their voice that turns my stomach. Because it feels like I'm being scolded and threatened at the same time. And I want to believe I can trust Fin; I just barged into their dimension because I believed that to my core. Only now, I'm not so sure.

"We're going to go after them, right?" My voice is shaky and small, and I almost feel like I'm low, but I'm not. Because low blood sugar doesn't exist in this dimension. Which should be the best thing I've heard since I got diabetes. But I want an explanation for why I feel this shaky and strange that isn't *I've made a truly terrible mistake and put my grandma in more danger when I was trying to save her.*

"We will," Fin says, setting Clío back down on the ground. "I know where they are likely to have taken them. Where all adult witches who enter this dimension are drawn. Even Cadwalader and Margaret will not be able to keep Orla and Patrick away from the pull for long."

"Cadwalader and Margaret?" I ask. "Those are the Mysteries' names?"

"Well, those are the versions of their names you can comprehend," Fin says.

"Fine, whatever," I say, trying to keep my anger from taking over my entire brain. "But you know where they'll go? And we can go there too?"

"Indeed," Fin says. "Though we'll need to take a different path, seeing as none of our assembled group has wings."

"I don't care what path it is! Fin!" And I fully give up on trying to stay calm because this is ridiculous. "Two Mystery demons just *flew away* with my grandma. The grandma I spent weeks trying to figure out how to rescue!"

"Weeks?" Fin tilts their head. "Weeks have already passed in your dimension?"

"That is so not the point here right now!"

Clío whines and paws at my leg.

"I'm sorry, girl," I say. "But Fin is being the actual literal worst."

The look on Fin's face is so offended and hurt I almost laugh.

"That is a low blow, Bernadette," they say. "I have met beings that qualify for such a title, and though I know my meandering mental cadences can be confounding, I am not the *literal* worst, and I'll thank you for taking that back."

"It's just an expression," I groan. "But you could earn

the actual title if you don't explain a lot of things really fast," I say. "While we're on our way to wherever those Mysteries are taking my grandma."

"I suppose that's fair," Fin says. Though they still look extremely offended. Which is absurd. But that's Fin.

CHAPTER TWENTY-SIX
i'm not at liberty to say

"Travel in this dimension can be strange," Fin explains as we set off through the forest. "Paths do not remain the same and locations are less relevant than intentions. You'll need to stay close. Especially you," they add, looking meaningfully at Clío and Mars. "Though, in case we're separated for any reason, it would be best if we were properly acquainted."

"This is Clío," I say. "It's short for Clíodhna. She's my diabetes alert dog."

"Lovely to meet you," Fin says, crouching down and staring into my dog's eyes for a long time. Or what feels like a long time. Maybe I'm just impatient about, well, everything.

"She cares for you very deeply," Fin says. "You are

lucky to have each other." There's something strange in their voice as they rise and start walking again. Something that feels a little bit like—

"Are you jealous?" I ask.

"I'm sure I have no idea what you mean," Fin huffs. Absolutely jealous.

"You don't like that I replaced you with a dog," I say.

"You most certainly did not, because I am irreplaceable," Fin says.

I almost make a joke. And then I almost tell them the truth, that that's true and they knew it and they still left me alone in the mortal dimension. Well, not alone, I guess. But they still left. And seeing them again is reminding me how little I know them. It's strange, how you can only know someone for a few days but feel like you've known them forever. Which reminds me.

"What was that about you and Grandma Orla knowing each other?"

"I'm not at liberty to say," Fin says.

"Really? Here in the demon dimension, you're not at liberty to say?" I can't help it, I roll my eyes. But it's not like anyone's here who would scold me about it.

"Most especially in the demon dimension," they say.

"But in this case, it's because I think your grandmother would prefer you hear her side of the story first."

"Side of the story?" I frown.

"Every story has multiple sides." Fin smiles.

"I thought you hated her," I say. "Grandma Orla. When you were in the mortal dimension. You seemed obsessed with her, and you . . . well, you basically stalked her at that equinox gathering. But why did you leave that message? I thought it was a spell, but it wasn't, was it?"

I feel like my questions are getting mixed up and messy, but if anyone can handle mixed up and messy, it's Fin.

"I didn't have much time to decide what to put in Cai's mind," Fin explains. "Human minds work so differently from ours. And Orla thought of that man, the one with the silly hat, the one who wrote the message. She thought of him when she saw me again. And I knew he knew of and believed in Mysteries. I could sense from her memory that he dabbled in other magics, that the two of them had a deep history—perhaps deeper even than ours had been."

And I'm not sure if they mean mine and theirs or theirs and Grandma Orla's, but I'm not about to interrupt.

"I could see him, that man, in her memories and in

her fear. Of me." Their voice goes all scratchy, and it almost seems like they're going to cry. I wonder if not crying in this dimension is a human thing or a thing for demons too.

"And in her fear," they continue, "suddenly a memory of hers made sense. A memory with a poem and a letter. And I knew there was a record of it in her house."

"But how did you see the memory?" I ask.

"She gave it to a Dismember," they say. "A long, long time ago."

"And you saw it?" I ask. "How?"

"I'm not—"

"At liberty to say," I finish, crossing my arms over my chest. "Well, okay, so you saw her memory before, but that night, in September. How did you know about her fear? Can you read her mind?"

I'd wondered if Fin could reach into our minds like Cai, or maybe even more literally than Cai. I knew they were holding back the extent of their power, but I didn't want to think too much about it at the time. And I'm not sure I even want to know.

"No," Fin says, shaking their head. "I can't read minds, not like your friend Cai." I'm not sure I entirely believe them and there's something in the way they won't look at me when they say it that doesn't exactly put out the little flickers of doubt sparking in my mind. "But," they continue, "because we knew each other before, because I know Orla's heart and mind better than I know most living witches—perhaps any living witches—I have a feeling, a sense for her mind. Particularly when it's quite loud. And it was very, very loud when confronted with the Cataclysm and taken hostage by that terrible coven."

"The terrible coven that's somewhere in this dimension, right?"

"Indeed," Fin agrees.

"Wait." I stop, suddenly remembering what Cai said when he arrived at Grandma Orla's house being chased by the flock of birds. It's hard to believe that was only a couple of hours ago. Though maybe it wasn't. I don't know how time passes here. I push that worry away for later, if there is a later.

"Is the Kalispell Coven hurting the Mysteries?" I ask. "Cai had a dream and—"

"Oh, no," Fin says. "They aren't causing any harm. At least—" They pause, looking up into the canopy of the trees as if listening to something far off I can't hear. "Well, at least none that I can sense."

"Then what did Cai see?" I ask. "He had a dream that you and Grandma Orla were fighting, and he said it seemed like the Kalispell Coven was hurting the Mysteries. And that you wanted us to come help you. That last part seems a little silly now," I add, feeling shame rising in my throat. "What help could a couple kids be in the demon dimension."

"Quite a lot of help," Fin says. "And I was sending Cai messages, but the dream wasn't part of that. I was seeking your help. I have been for a long time, in fact." They cross their arms and frown. "It is quite possible that Cai glimpsed a disagreement between Orla and myself. She was rather tiresome when we first arrived, and even more irksome thereafter."

"Fin!" I groan. "You're not explaining anything."

"I'm explaining what is worthy of explanation, or capable of being articulated," they say. "I can't say for certain what Cai saw, though I can assure you the Kalispell Coven has caused no harm here outside of acute consternation."

"Conster-what?" I ask. I thought this dimension didn't have bodily functions.

"Confusion, befuddlement, mental anguish or alarm," Fin explains. "Which is not painful or harmful. In fact, confusion, befuddlement, and consternation were once the core of a blood witch's purpose in this dimension." They raise their eyebrow ridges, waggling them ridiculously. "You know, when witches visited this dimension with more regularity, you served a very particular purpose."

"Which was?" I ask, though I'm 99.99 percent sure what Fin's response will be.

And right on cue, they say, "I'm not . . ." They trail off, frowning in concentration. "Well, I'm not certain you will like the answer to that question," they finish, and then they keep walking, and I have no choice but to follow.

CHAPTER TWENTY-SEVEN
the bamboozle ballet

I've never had an especially good grasp on time. Not even with my insulin pump, which has a built-in clock. It's always felt like the more I try to pay attention to time, the wonkier it gets—shifting and distorting until what I thought would take five minutes has eaten hours, or what I thought would take all day is done in just a minute.

But if I thought my understanding of time was bad back in the mortal dimension, I can't even begin to guess at how much time is (or isn't) passing in the demon dimension. Fin seems to be both in a hurry and entirely laid-back. Which is infuriatingly normal. If they're not being contradictory, they aren't being Fin.

As we've walked, the trees have changed. As in, we

are walking through parts of the strange forest with trees that look different and also that I'm watching the trees change right in front of my eyes. They're more spread apart now, and every color imaginable. Some are even colors I'm certain I couldn't imagine—or maybe even see—in the mortal dimension. They're now squat and roundish, like the bottom part of a really bushy Christmas tree, but without a pointy top.

"How far do we have to go?" I ask, and when Fin doesn't answer right away, I add, "You do know where we're going, right?"

"No one actually knows where they're going in this dimension, Bernadette," they say. "And distance is relative."

"Well, my relative is waiting at the end of that unknown distance," I snap. "And I would very much like to know we're at least making progress."

My anger is suddenly so close to the surface that I almost check my pump, wondering if my blood sugar is high. But then I remember, it can't be. I don't have blood sugar here. I actually haven't had to think about my blood sugar at all. And won't need to, as long as I'm here.

And I think that's another reason why time feels so strange here. It's only been half a year since I was diagnosed, but diabetes takes up a huge portion of my thoughts most of the time. For the few days Fin was with me in the mortal dimension in September, the amount of brain I needed to use to think about diabetes decreased a ton. And it's just not the same with a pump and CGM, even though they're great. They're still a *lot* to think about. A million decisions I have to make every day. But as long as I'm in the demon dimension, I'm not a diabetic anymore.

I almost laugh at the thought, and based on the feeling in my chest and throat, tears would be filling my eyes if I had tears in this dimension. The realization that I'm just a normal blood witch—at least for now—is such a relief it almost becomes stressful in a strange way, so I try to think about anything else.

"Is this a planet?" I ask.

"Not a planet, no." Fin scratches Clío's ears. I hadn't realized they'd scooped her up, but she's draped over their shoulder, tongue lolling happily out of her mouth, ears perked. I wait for Fin to explain more, but they don't, and I decide not to push it. I'm not sure I'd be able to understand their explanation if they offered it and it's kind of nice to sort through my own thoughts for a few minutes as we walk.

I've also noticed that I don't get tired in this dimension. Not tired. No diabetes. No sweat. I definitely don't have to pee. My period! Do I still have my period?

I haven't felt any uncomfortable wetness, but I still feel the bulk of my pad. For a second, I almost ask Fin, but immediately decide against it. Cai took the shame away from talking about my period, but I think it could find a way to creep back in if I brought it up to Fin. Or if not shame, at least awkwardness I could avoid by just not saying anything. But thinking of Cai reminds me of a question I do want to ask.

"Why couldn't Cai and Phoebe come with us? You said something about only blood witches being able to come to the demon dimension, but why? Wait, let me guess, you're not at liberty to say."

"In fact, it's worse than that," Fin says. "I don't know."

"Wait, seriously?"

"Unfortunately, yes." Their tail reaches up and tickles Clío's nose. She chomps at it playfully.

"Be gentle," I say to her automatically.

"Oh, she needn't worry," Fin says. "It can regenerate."

I think they mean their tail. And I absolutely don't want to think about that. Thankfully, I don't have to. Couldn't even if I tried. Because right at that moment, we round a corner, and a huge waterfall blocks the path. Except I'm not sure it's water. It's frothing and orange and absolutely moving from the ground up over the cliff high above us. And then I see the demons.

Hundreds of demons soar around the frothing

orange—I'm just going to call it water, because I need something I can see that I can just identify as the thing I think it might be.

The demons all have metallic feathers and fur and shine in the sherbet-colored mist. They're all about the size of pugs, and their feathers and fur are tons of shades of metallic brown, from deep bronze to shimmering, bright gold.

As far as I can see, they all have hooked beaks that are obsidian black, which match their long, long, sharp claws on their four paws and the tip of each wing. And I know these demons.

"Bamboozles," I whisper.

"A Bamboozle Ballet," Fin says. "A very lucky sighting. They actually mostly sleep, but occasionally they gather and it's quite a spectacle, is it not?"

I've seen Bamboozles before, I'm familiar with Bamboozles. I didn't think I was scared of Bamboozles. But I've never seen more of them than I can count swirl into a flashing cloud and begin to dart in and out of an epic inverse waterfall.

"Yeah," I agree. "It's . . . a lot."

Several of the Bamboozles branch off and soar up over the cliff, higher and higher until they are only tiny specks. And then they dive back down with furious and terrifying speed. I reach for Mars instinctively, but he's glued in place on my shoulder, watching the demons with narrowed eyes—utterly unbothered. I tear my gaze away from the spectacle of the Bamboozles doing what looks like actual, honest-to-goddess choreography—their thick fuzzy legs and shimmering wings forming complicated shapes as they dive in and out of the water—to check on my poor dog. Who looks . . . thrilled? Her tongue is still hanging out of her mouth and she's practically smiling as she gazes around at the Mayhem demons. Well, I'm not gonna question that too much. Maybe she thinks they're just flying, sparkly dogs. Flying, sparkly dogs who are currently forming a shining, furious tornado.

And then the air starts to shimmer to the left of the waterfall and several of the Bamboozles let out loud screeches, breaking formation and disappearing.

"What the—"

"Ah, unfortunate timing," Fin says. "The formation is completely asymmetrical without those three."

"What happened?" I ask.

"Well, they were conjured," Fin says. "By a blood witch."

"Oh," I say. Of course. Demons are conjured from the demon dimension to fulfill purposes in the mortal dimension. This is where they're coming from. "Does it hurt?" I ask.

"Did it hurt when you moved between dimensions?" Fin counters.

I think about it for a moment. It wasn't exactly comfortable. But it didn't hurt.

I shake my head. "It was strange, but not painful."

"That is similar to what they experience too." Relief rushes through me, but then they add, "But if you found out it caused pain, would you stop conjuring?"

"Yes," I say automatically. "Of course."

"Really?" Fin asks. "What if it was only a small amount of pain, like stubbing your toe?"

"Stubbing your toe can hurt a *lot*," I say.

"Or it can only hurt a little," Fin says. "I don't technically have toes, so I can't actually say from experience, but humans are always bashing into things."

"I mean, some more than others," I mutter.

"But say it hurt as much as . . . testing your blood sugar," they say. "You knew that conjuring an Anecdote meant it would hurt it the same amount it hurt you. Would you still conjure?"

"I . . . I don't know." And it's true. I don't. I hadn't considered it before.

"A life without conjuring would be strange for a blood witch," Fin says. "It would mean giving up a lot of what makes you, you. It's why that Lindley woman who leads the profaning coven started sacrificing blood that didn't belong to her, blood that wasn't hers to give. Because giving up power is difficult."

Fin's dark black eyes meet mine and the intensity in their gaze is almost painful. Because I don't know what to think about this. They just said it doesn't cause the demons pain to be conjured, but what if it did? And we definitely don't pause to ask a demon what they're doing in this dimension before we conjure them. Even if we could, would we?

"Just something to think about, little witch," Fin says.

I nod. Because I'm not sure I can trust my voice. It's like there's a fist around my heart and my brain feels too big for my skull. I don't want to hurt anyone ever. But then I remember the Devilry I conjured to mess with Krystal. I didn't want her to get hurt, I just wanted her to feel . . . what?

I guess I wanted her to feel what I felt. I wanted her to feel small. I wanted her to feel wrong. I wanted her to feel bad because she made me feel bad. And that's pain, isn't it?

"I didn't mean to set off an existential crisis," Fin says, reaching out a hand and patting the shoulder Mars isn't sitting on.

"What's an existential crisis?" I ask.

"Exactly," Fin says. "Now, you're going to need to climb on my back for this next bit."

"Wait, what?" I ask. "And more importantly, how? I have Clío and Mars."

"I will carry the canine as well. Mars will not fall as long as you do not."

"Yeah, um, that isn't making me feel much better about this," I say.

"Well, your feelings are rather outside my control," Fin says. "But your safety is not, so please, climb up." They point to a rock and then to their back.

I very much do not want to go on a Mystery demon piggyback ride up a cliff, but what are the other options? So I climb onto the rock and then wrap my arms around Fin's neck when they crouch down slightly. I've barely got my legs wrapped around their waist when they rise up. I don't even have time to tell them to take it slow before they absolutely do not take anything slow at all.

I cling to their neck, grabbing my own wrists like I've seen cheerleaders do with each other when they do pyramids. And then Fin is scaling the cliff. At first, I squeeze my eyes shut and cling on for dear life. But after a few seconds, I realize that it's not actually that hard to hold on. I'm not about to let go, but I don't need to be clinging quite so desperately. And then I decide to chance it and open my eyes.

And when I look to my right, I see dozens of Bamboozles still swirling around the frothing orange water. They are beautiful and terrifying and look like they're having an absolute blast. And I can't believe it, but I'm smiling. Fin races up the cliff and even though I'm not really great with heights, I decide to look down.

For a second my vision swims, because we are *really* high up. But then I let the forest come into focus and it's beautiful. The multicolored trees stretch as far as I can see, denser and taller in some places and spread out in others. In the far distance they seem to tower as high as the cliff. Or maybe that's another cliff. Maybe we were in a valley. The sky is less lavender now, shifting to mauve.

"Is it sunset?" I ask Fin, raising my voice over the rushing of the water and the flapping of the Bamboozles' wings.

"No sun to set," Fin says. "The sky just does that."

"Cool," I say.

"Indeed, little witch," Fin says. "It really, truly is."

And then we're at the top of the cliff, on solid ground. More solid than the ground at the bottom of it, that's for sure. So solid that my knees feel a little funny, like when you get off a boat onto dry land and you feel like the ground *should* be moving like water for a bit.

"What's the opposite of sea legs?" I ask.

"Land legs," Fin answers. And I'm not sure they understood what I was really asking, but they aren't technically wrong.

The land stretching out before us doesn't look like

land at all. It looks like the orange water. And that's because it is. I think?

"What is this?" I ask, looking down at my feet. They're covered in orange, frothy liquid but don't feel wet.

"The Expanse," Fin says. And when I look up at them, they're gesturing out across the . . . well, expanse. The land stretches out before us as far as I can see, orange-sherbet-colored froth on the ground, and mauve above in the sky. And far, far in the distance, they meet.

"I meant the orange stuff," I say. "But yeah, the Expanse seems like a pretty solid name for wherever we are."

"It's actually not solid at all," Fin says. "As you can see." They bend and scoop up some of the orange froth and take a little sip out of their hands before gesturing like I should do the same.

"Um, I'm good," I say.

"I agree," Fin says with a nod and a smile before setting off through the ankle-deep foam, Clío still draped over their shoulder.

I pause, looking back at the forest at the bottom of the cliff. For all Fin's talk about this dimension being strange to navigate, they sure do seem certain about which direction to head in. And that should be reassuring. This is their dimension, after all. But something inside me is whispering something I can't understand.

And that something feels like it's directions. Which is nonsense. It has to be. I've never been to the demon dimension. I have no idea where we should be going or how we could get there. So why does it feel like I know exactly which way we should go? And that it's not the direction Fin is headed in.

CHAPTER TWENTY-EIGHT

the weird compass bubble situation

I trail after Fin at a bit of a distance. For a while I think they're going to slow down so I can catch up. But they don't. They also never get quite far enough away for me to truly fall behind. I use it as an opportunity to collect my thoughts. Or try to. My brain feels like a flimsy plastic grocery bag with a hole in it, dropping my thoughts out of it like oranges and apples and packs of ramen noodles. Bang, thwap, splat, thump.

It's clear Grandma Orla and Fin have history. It's also clear Fin doesn't want to talk about that history. Or maybe they do, but they feel like Grandma Orla will want me to hear something else. But why do they care what Grandma Orla wants or thinks all of a sudden? Back in September when they were in the mortal dimension, they seemed like they hated Grandma Orla, and all Crowleys.

Well, except me, I guess.

And why did they leave me those clues and bring me to the demon dimension to begin with if the Kalispell Coven isn't wreaking havoc here? Why didn't they just send Grandma Orla home? I can't shake the feeling there's something going on here that I'm not seeing. Literally or figuratively. Because all I can see is the Expanse. Endless orange foam and Fin about twenty yards ahead of me, my dog still draped over their shoulder.

"Do you trust them?" I ask Mars.

He purrs and nestles into my neck.

"Of course you do," I say. "You trusted them since I first bound them."

And so did you, a part of my brain reminds me. I firmly remind it that I'm wrong about a lot of things. And being wrong about whether I can trust Fin or not could mean never getting back to the human dimension at all.

I expect that thought to scare me, but it doesn't. Which is scary in its own way. Because this isn't so bad. It's strange, sure. But the Bamboozles were actually pretty cool. I have Mars and Clío. And Fin. But it's what I don't have that is really the most important factor here: I don't have diabetes. And that shouldn't be enough for me to consider abandoning my entire family and dimension, but if I'm completely and totally honest with myself, there's a tiny part of me—probably my dead pancreas—that might just make that trade.

That thought freaks me out so much that I hurry to catch up with Fin. Being alone with your thoughts for a second is great, until they turn on you.

When I finally reach Fin, they're muttering to Clío in what I think is Irish. And then I realize they aren't muttering, they're singing.

"You can sing?" The question is out of my mouth before I can think better of it.

"All beings sing, in their way," Fin says when they finish the verse. Or maybe chorus. It's not a song I recognize. But Clío seems to like it.

They keep singing, and though it's eerily soothing, I can't stop the doubt building in my chest. It almost feels like a physical thing, just under my heart. It's like a bubble is growing there and it's tugging me away from Fin. Not back toward the cliff. At least I don't think so. But not in the direction we're headed either.

"Are you sure we're headed the right way?" I ask.

They stop singing. Then they stop walking. Their head tilts to the side as if they're considering the question.

"I thought I'd have longer," they say. And whatever I expected, it wasn't that. Because that's not even remotely an answer to my question. It's practically a fountain spouting other questions.

"Have longer for what?" I ask, even though I'm a tiny bit afraid of the answer.

"They're calling to you, aren't they?" Fin asks.

"What do you mean?" I ask, even though I'm pretty sure they're somehow aware of the weird compass bubble situation happening in my ribs.

"Your memories," Fin says. "It happens to all grown witches when they linger in this dimension. They are drawn to the memories they've sent here before them. I thought it would perhaps take longer, since you are not yet technically of age. But human measurements of age and time are always fickle and fallible, and you know yourself very well for someone so young."

"Fin, what are you talking about?"

"You're being drawn to the Memorabilia. It's where your grandmother will be. And probably the Kalispell Coven by this stage."

"What's the Memorabilia?" I ask.

"You'll see soon enough," Fin says. "But it's where your memories go when they are surrendered to Dismembers."

"Wait," I say, my brain reeling. "Hold up, our memories come *here* when we give them to a Dismember?"

Fin doesn't reply, but lifts Clío above their head.

"What the heck, Fin?" I ask, looking around to see if there's some demon headed for us or if the foam is rising or something. But all I see is the Expanse.

"I'm holding her aloft, per your instructions," Fin explains.

"Fin, it's just an expression," I say. "I wanted you to slow down and explain what you're saying about memories and Dismembers and the Memora—whatever."

"Memorabilia," Fin says. "It was part of our original bargain with blood witches centuries ago. When our mutual sacrifices were agreed upon to preserve the balance between dimensions. Sacrifice of blood and sacrifice of memories. They each serve different purposes.

"Memories are actually the most powerful sacrifices you make as blood witches. Much more powerful than piddly little drops of blood. And, well, the beings of this dimension that you call Awarenesses, Buffers, Confusions, and Dismembers—Memory demons—are . . . collectors of sorts. You might call them curators, historians, even. So every memory they've ever taken from your dimension is stored in . . ." They trail off.

"The Memorabilia," I finish. My mind races. The memories I've given to Dismembers over the years are here? Somewhere? Does that mean I could get them back?

"Though your kind have gotten a great deal wrong

about the beings of this dimension," Fin continues, "you are most often wrong in the 'tomato is technically a fruit' kind of way and not in the 'two plus two is five' kind of way. Though two plus two can equal five in certain circumstances, of course."

"Of course," I say, mostly because I have other much more important questions and I'm certain that there is no dimension where two plus two equals five. "But why didn't you want me to get to the Memorabilia?" I ask.

"I, well, I wasn't ready."

"Why?" The tugging in my chest feels stronger than ever, and it's almost like it's fighting with my need to understand why Fin didn't actually want me going to Grandma Orla. Especially if I was the one who could lead us there. "Why, Fin? Why didn't you want me to find my grandma?" I ask. "And my memories?" I add, my voice shaking.

"Because I'm rather proud, Bernadette," Fin says. "I do care quite a lot what you think of me. And I fear when you see the memories waiting for you in the Memorabilia, when you see the truth of my history with your family . . . Well, I'm quite concerned your opinion of me will plummet and that you will understand the Crowley hatred of all Mysteries, and of me in particular." They turn away, dropping their head. "And I had hoped, while we are out of time, to charm you a bit more and perhaps secure you as a true ally, in the way your namesake once was. Before I ruined everything."

Before *Fin* ruined everything? Secure me as an ally? My mind is on hyper-speed, but it screeches to a halt as it settles on one particular thing Fin said.

"Out of time?" I squeak. "Are we out of time? Out of time to do what?"

"Oh, my dear witch, I mean that literally," Fin says, turning back to me and taking my hand in theirs. "This dimension is not subject to the passage of time, which was part of my mistake, my misunderstanding."

"Fin, where is my grandma? Where is the Kalispell Coven? What am I doing in this dimension?"

"I hope you are helping me right a wrong," Fin says. "But in order to do that, we'll both have to face our pasts."

"I don't understand," I say.

"And neither did I," Fin says. And I want to pull my hand from theirs and throttle them. Because this is ridiculous.

"Fin, please, can we just go find Grandma Orla?" I plead. "Can you tell me how to find her?"

"Yes," Fin says, and I want to cry I'm so relieved. But of course, I don't. I almost wish I could. It would be a release of everything building inside me since I've been in this dimension.

"But first, I need you to understand a few things, okay?"

"Are they even things I *can* understand?" I ask. "Because you keep talking in circles, Fin. And now you tell me you were literally leading me in the wrong direction. I just don't know what to think anymore."

"Blood witches used to come to the demon dimension regularly," Fin says. And just when I think they're finally explaining things, they go and say something so absurd that I actually think I might have left my brain in the mortal dimension. Because what Fin says next is too ridiculous for a human brain to accept.

"Blood witches from the most powerful families almost all came to this dimension," Fin repeats. "But you came here as babies."

CHAPTER TWENTY-NINE

an unauthorized field trip

"Very funny," I say. But I'm not laughing. And neither is Fin.

"I do not jest," Fin says. "Well, I do. Quite often, actually. But that was not a jest. It was a fact. For many generations, blood witches sent their young witches—when they were still squishy and silly and utterly delightful little chaos gremlins—to come entertain a Mystery for a time. In exchange, we served them in the mortal dimension for a time."

"Entertain?" I splutter.

"Indeed," Fin says. They sigh, as if imparting truly terrible information. "That is the only purpose your kind serve in this dimension I'm afraid. Though"—they hold out their hands—"it is a very essential and wonderful purpose. One we cherish enough to use our considerable magic and power in your dimension."

"You're seriously telling me blood witches just sent their babies and toddlers into another dimension to be looked after by demons?" I fully cannot process this information. And maybe I just won't.

"Well, I wasn't trying to be overly serious about it, no." Fin crosses their arms. "But yes, Mysteries have a fondness for the youngest of your kind, and we are quite wonderful caretakers. Particularly when food and water and waste disposal are not requisite."

"Wait, is that how you know Grandma Orla?" I demand. "Did you—was she—did her mom send—" I can't even finish the question but Fin nods.

"Orla's mother bound me," Fin says. "And I brought Orla to this dimension. However—" They break off and look away. "Well, though time doesn't exist here, it does exist in another dimension. A dimension that is not the mortal dimension. A dimension where I took Orla for what you might call . . . an unauthorized field trip."

"To another dimension?"

Mars squirms on my shoulder and Clío jumps down from Fin's shoulder and runs to me through the orange foam.

"I'm sorry, girl," I say. "I'm just a little bit upset." I glare at Fin.

"As was your namesake," Fin says. "I didn't understand what I had done until it was far too late. But when I returned to the mortal dimension, expecting to find Orla's mother and complete my service to her in your dimension, well . . ." They trail off again, and when they look back at me, their eyes are so full of sadness and regret it almost hurts to look at them.

"I didn't realize I'd taken a toddler into the demon dimension and brought back a little girl," Fin says. "We don't perceive time in the same way and can't detect the changes in human forms very well. Ordinarily we can enjoy the company of a tiny blood witch indefinitely and bring them back to the mortal dimension unchanged but enriched by their time here. But that was not the case when I brought Orla . . . elsewhere."

"How much time had passed?" I ask. "For my family? How much time had passed in the mortal dimension?"

"Four years," Fin says. "And—" They shake their head like they can't bear to finish the sentence.

"And what, Fin?" I growl. I'm trying to imagine what it must have felt like for Grandma Orla's mom to lose four years of her daughter's life.

"And her mother had died," Fin says. "While Orla and I had been away, Niamh had died."

My heart freezes. I knew Grandma Orla had lost her mom when she was young, but I hadn't realized she hadn't even been there. Because of course I hadn't. Because I didn't know anything about any of this.

"Your great-great-grandmother was furious," Fin says. "And I didn't understand. She swore to never bind another Mystery, to never send another blood witch child to the demon dimension. And I was foolish, so foolish. I didn't believe she'd do it. I didn't believe she'd conjure a dozen Dismembers. But she did." They sink to their knees and drop their head into their hands. "And before I could stop her, she forgot—all of it. She sacrificed every memory she'd had of our friendship, of the balance, of blood witches' true connection to Mysteries. And she's been ensuring everyone else forgets ever since. Until you."

Fin falls silent and I stand there for a long time. Clío whines at my feet, but I ignore her. I need a second—or maybe a year—to process what Fin's just said.

Fin stole years of Grandma Orla's life from her family. No wonder Great-Great-Grandma Ber didn't want anyone binding a Mystery ever again.

"That's why I didn't want you to reach the Memorabilia too soon," Fin says. "Because I'm not certain what the Crowley version of those memories holds—the version of me trapped in them."

"Then let's find out," I say. My voice is strange and flat, and I don't even know what to feel anymore.

"We're going to the Memorabilia."

"Yes," Fin agrees as they push themself to standing. "I do believe we are. And, if you're willing, I know a shortcut. But it's not for the faint of heart."

"Is it really a shortcut?" I snap. "Or is it another trick?"

"It is really unsettling," Fin says. "But I swear upon the Great Mystery itself that I'm not willfully deceiving you in any way, and that if we proceed through the Squelch, we will reach the Memorabilia imminently."

"Does imminently mean soon?" I ask.

"Soonest," Fin says. "For we are very near to the Squelch, indeed."

I thought that maybe Fin was being, well, Fin, when they said "very near to," and that we'd actually have a Void, a Swathe, and a Vastness to cross before we got to the Squelch. But in what feels like no time at all, the Expanse ends, and we reach an endless wall of . . . flowers?

"So, what did you mean by 'really unsettling'?" I ask as I look at the waving wall of pink. It stretches as far as I can see in every direction, and I'm baffled how I didn't notice it as we approached. It's covered in about a million flowers in every shade of pink, from bubble gum to magenta.

"Are we talking scary? Difficult? Literally something else I'd never think of because your vocabulary is light-years ahead of mine even though it seems like it's your twenty-seventh language or something?"

Fin either doesn't hear me or doesn't care to explain. Instead, they study the wall, an expression on their face I can't place.

"Um, Fin?" I finally ask. "Did you hear me?"

"One hundred and seventeenth," Fin says.

"What?"

"English was my one hundred and seventeenth language," they explain.

"Seriously?"

"Rarely," Fin replies. "I find English is particularly useful for a great many emotions, but there are at least twelve languages I'd choose for all things serious before English."

I can't tell if they're joking, which I think is their point.

"In a moment, we'll step into the Squelch, Bernadette. And I just need you to remember that even if you get the sensation that you are being squashed, stretched, or even perhaps dismembered, you are not. It's an illusion of sorts. A side effect of this mode of transport."

"A side effect?" I squeak. "I might feel like I'm being dismembered!? Like literally? Physically? Not the Memory sacrifice kind? Like the limbs coming off kind?"

"It might feel like it, yes," Fin says. "But not in a painful way."

"There's a type of limbs ripping off that isn't painful?"

"Well, yes, when your limbs are not, in fact, being removed."

"What about Mars?" I ask. "And Clío?"

"Cats are not, in fact, solid, as you know. So Mars will be unaffected."

"And my dog!?"

"I will carry her and shield her from the worst of the Squelch's disorienting effects." Fin looks down at me. "Or perhaps we should take a longer route. Maybe you aren't quite Squelch material."

"I don't even want to know what you mean by that," I mutter. "But don't act like you know me. You don't. And it turns out I don't know you very well at all either."

"Well, that could be true," Fin says. "There are many mysteries still between us."

"Then let's go find some answers," I say, gesturing at the wall of flowers.

"This next bit is going to be a bit disorienting," Fin says.

"Because everything so far has been so orienting?" I ask.

"By comparison, yes," Fin says. My stomach tightens

at their tone. Whatever's coming next must be next-level weird if it warrants this many warnings.

I take a deep breath as I get Mars settled on my shoulder. How bad can it be? I regret that question as soon as I think it. But there's really no turning back now. Besides, I faced a Cataclysm and a dozen Butcheries in the mortal dimension. I can handle whatever illusions the Squelch has in store. And the sensation of being squashed and stretched and—okay, not going to think about it anymore.

"Let's go," I say. "Less thinking, more going."

"What a very human thing to say," Fin says. But they scoop up my dog and vanish into the wall of flowers. I take a breath—or whatever I've been doing that feels like breathing but is not actually breathing in this dimension—and step forward. And hope with all my heart that whatever this Squelch has in store doesn't last too long.

CHAPTER THIRTY
the squelch

There's a moment when I first step into the flowers after Fin that I think they've exaggerated. The sensation of the petals brushing my face is pleasant, almost tickling, but not quite. Then there's a squeeze, like a weighted blanket is being dropped on me from all sides. And it's comforting. Like the most perfect hug in the universe.

And then it all changes.

For how obsessed they are with words, Fin's description of the effects of the Squelch fell very, very short. But maybe that's because there are no words. There are no directions. No sensations. But I feel everything. At the same time, I am nothing. I'm pizza crust being eaten by a ravenous raccoon. I'm the last mozzarella stick in the basket that's gone a bit cold, and I break instead of stretching like my friends before me. I'm the sugar-free gum on the bottom of Krystal with a K's perfectly white shoes as she walks across the lunchroom of the universe, and I feel every. Single. Step.

I'm turning to absurdist poetry. I'm losing my mind. Literally. It's being pulled from my skull, and I'll never think another thought. Which is a relief, but only for a moment. Because I need my mind. There's something I have to do. Someone I used to be.

There's something in my ear. It's wet.

And there's something on my nose. It's scratchy.

"Bernadette?" A musical tenor voice with a slight Irish lilt cuts through the oatmeal where my brain used to be. "Bernadette?" the voice repeats.

Fin. It's Fin.

I blink my eyes open.

I'm on the ground. Mars is perched on my chest, licking my face. Guess that's what the scratchiness on my nose was. I turn my head just in time for Clío to go in for another ear lick and instead slobber directly onto my lips.

"Why yes, that was rather effective, well done, you two," Fin says as I splutter and wipe the dog saliva from my mouth.

"If there aren't tears in this dimension, why is there slobber?" I groan as I sit up.

"It appears that dog drool defies interdimensional laws and logistics," Fin says.

"I mean, that tracks." I accept the hand Fin is holding

out and let them pull me to standing. "Are we wherever we're supposed to be?"

"Indeed," Fin affirms. "Can you feel the pull?"

"The pull—?" I start to ask, but the question dissolves on my tongue. Because yes, I can. The weird bubble compass in the center of my chest is urging me in a very particular direction.

"Whoa." My legs go wobbly for a second and I almost feel like I'm back in the Squelch.

"Let's sit for just a moment," Fin says. "Not a delay, a recalibration."

"Fine," I say, because I'm not sure I can trust my legs quite yet.

Fin leads me to what appears to be a large black rock, but instead of sitting on it, they nudge it. It quickly becomes clear that it is very much not a rock at all. I have no idea what it is. It doesn't resemble anything I've ever seen in Intermediate Principles or on iDemon. Whatever it is slowly unravels, stretching and morphing before settling into what is unmistakably a bench.

They sit down, patting the place next to them.

"We can sit on . . . them?" I ask uncertainly.

"It," Fin says. "Not entirely sentient, though very comfortable."

I don't even try to fully process that and collapse onto the not-entirely-sentient-being bench next to them.

Like everything else in this dimension, it squishes. It's unnervingly comfortable. Mars climbs from my arms and drapes himself over the back of the benchlike being, purring loudly. Clío jumps up next to me and we all sit in purr-lulled almost silence. To our left is the innocent-looking Squelch, pink flowers still gently waving. But everywhere the wall of flowers isn't, is sand. Golden, sandy hills. There is a cluster of buildings on the top of one in the near distance, and I wonder if that's the Memorabilia. But I check in with the new, unnerving compass in my chest, and no.

"Is she okay?" I ask Fin as I scritch Clío's ears. "After the Squelch?"

"I think you're a better judge of that than I," Fin says. "Does she seem her normal self?"

I lean over, looking into her furry ginger face.

"You okay, girl?" I ask.

She licks my nose.

"I'm going to take that as a yes," I say.

"Then perhaps we should be on our way," Fin says. They rise off the not-quite-sentient bench and stretch. As I stand, I realize I don't actually need to follow them. The pull inside me is insistent and growing stronger. And as we make our way around the edge of the nearest sandy hill, we appear to be on some sort of established path.

"Mars should be fine to walk on his own for now,"

Fin says. "Because we've arrived. I told you it was imminent if we braved the Squelch." They stretch out a long, elegant arm, gesturing ahead as we fully round the edge of a particularly steep and shimmery hill.

Before us, a huge glass bubble rises out of the golden sand.

The Memorabilia.

Wisps of red and deep purple zoom in and out of the roof, where I think there must be a hole or some sort of exit. Definitely Dismembers.

"Why's it so quiet?" I ask.

"Your pitiful human senses cannot perceive the fullness of the Memorabilia. If you had the additional 3.7 senses I possess, you might be able to comprehend the amalgam of sensory inputs bombarding us at this very moment."

"Um, translation?" I ask. Though I file *amalgam* away to look up when I'm studying for the PSATs this spring.

"It's loud, and emotionally dense, even if you cannot perceive either."

"Got it," I say. I want to ask what emotionally dense means, but then I decide I'm not sure I actually want to know. Curiosity and the cat and all that. The thought makes my heart clench as I glance around for Mars. But he's trotting alongside Fin, green eyes wide and fluffy tail held aloft. Clío is stuck to my side like a burr, and I wonder if whatever Fin meant by "emotionally dense" is affecting her. She still seems confused about the whole lack of blood sugar thing. And she's not alone. This dimension is a lot for anyone to take in.

We're in the shadow of the Memorabilia now. Or we would be, if it had a shadow.

"Oh dear," Fin says. "Well, the Kalispell Coven is here all right."

"They are? Is Grandma Orla?" I follow Fin's gaze through the wide arched gateway to the Memorabilia. The dome seems even bigger on the inside, somehow. There are spiraling ramps and so many shelves and landings it would be impossible to count them all. Everything is the same translucent almost-blue glass.

There are streaks of purple and red everywhere as Dismembers flit around the huge space. They're more substantial here. And then I see the Buffers. Actually see them, not just hints of forms in the corners of my eyes like they are in the mortal dimension. There are little blue Buffers of every shade scattered around. They are fuzzy and range in size from tiny little golf-ball-sized poofs to shaggy blobs that look like animated beanbag chairs. And they don't seem to have discernible heads or limbs.

There's one about ten feet to our right, draped over what looks like an intake desk at a library. And it looks . . . sad? Somehow? I don't know how I can tell, but that Buffer is definitely depressed. Maybe even forlorn. Three smaller demons flit around it, pale yellow, birdlike beings that I'm pretty sure are Awarenesses. At least, most Awarenesses are yellow in the mortal dimension.

But then a reddish-brown demon with too many limbs to count and at least five faces ambles up to us, and all my thoughts go mushy. Great. A Confusion. At least Fin seems relieved and crouches down to chat with it.

I strain to hear what they're saying, but then Clío bites my sleeve and tugs.

"Is it Grandma Orla?" I ask, before I realize she only met Grandma Orla for two seconds when we first landed in the demon dimension. But I can't keep my thoughts focused. I can't even remember what I thought Clío was trying to get me to see or find or realize. This is why we almost never conjure Confusions. They are just as likely to influence the conjuring witch as anyone they're conjured to confuse. Not that any of these demons were conjured. This is where they live, or exist?

"What is this place?" I mumble, mostly to myself. I fully don't expect an answer, but then a musical chime sounds as I approach the Buffer and its swirling Awarenesses and the counter it's sat upon.

"Welcome to the Memorabilia," a disembodied sing-song voice says. "Please describe the human emotion you'd like to experience today, as best as you are able, in whatever language or communication style is most comfortable for you."

CHAPTER THIRTY-ONE

the memorabilia

"Wait, what?" I ask, and I swear the Buffer sighs, rolls over, and without arms or hands or a face, it fully judges me and indicates a plaque on the desk. It's a directory. Like at a movie theater, or—then it hits me. A library. That's what this strange, magical space reminds me of. And this Buffer is definitely a librarian of sorts.

I scan the list in front of me, but it's not written in English, despite the melodic voice from a moment before. The Buffer sighs—again, without a mouth or face—and rolls slightly, revealing the list in English.

For All Audiences:
Pets & Pet-Like Animals

This is our most popular category; please respect strict viewing limits so as not to corrupt the memories.

Sadness, Longing & Other Human Angst

This is our second most popular category; may elicit an approximation of human empathy when viewed repeatedly. Proceed with caution, but single viewings are generally safe.

Suspense & Fear

This category is without Violence; please see "Mature Audiences" offerings for anything truly dramatic. Limit: one viewing per visit.

Friendship, Romance & Love

This includes cuddling, courtship traditions, and human bonding; please see the "Mature Audiences" category for mating rituals.

Humor

Please note that human expressions of humor vary vastly by culture and often do not reflect our understanding of the concept; all complaints are to be directed to the curators and not the floor staff.

And then there are a few more categories listed under another heading.

For Mature Audiences Only:
Trials & Tribulations
Elementary & Primary School Band Concerts
Expressions of Human Pair Bonding
Nostalgia, Violence & Regrets

I tear my eyes away from the list before I can think too much about that final category. Because these are human memories. Blood witch memories. Some of them are my memories.

"Um, thanks," I say to the Buffer before rushing back to Fin. They're gazing up, eyebrow ridges drawn together in concern.

"These are memories," I say. "Human memories."

"Yes," Fin says. Their voice is dreamy, distant. I wonder if the Confusion had an effect on them too. "This is the foremost collection of all the memories fed to Dismembers. Well, most of them. Occasionally a memory goes missing or goes bad. Gets twisted beyond recognition from overwatch."

"You're watching our memories for fun?" My voice is high, and heat rises in my cheeks. I can't remember what memories I've chosen to give to the Dismembers over the years, that's kind of the point. The memories are gone. But I guess I never imagined they were for someone else's entertainment.

"Well, fun isn't always the intended outcome," Fin says. "Just as with human entertainments in your dimension. Do you watch Shakespeare for fun? Is entertainment the same as fun? There are a great many things that are interesting that would fall outside what I would designate as—"

"But our memories are demon entertainment?" I can't even care that I've used the wrong word. Though I know I should. I don't know exactly why this place has me so unsettled. But the idea of things I can't remember—things I chose to forget—being watched by someone else makes my skin crawl. Almost in the same way as the idea of blood witch babies being bartered with for magical power.

"Memory demons are curators of human experience," Fin says. "The Memorabilia has been our primary connection to the mortal dimension since your namesake ensured Mysteries were no longer bound and blood witches no longer came to our dimension. But the Memorabilia is a reverent place. Almost like a library or museum in your dimension. We have a great deal of respect for, and interest in, what you chose to forget."

"What now?" I ask.

"Follow your instincts," Fin says.

"What?" I blink a few times, my mind finally clearing. The Confusion must have moved on.

"Don't think too poorly of me," Fin continues, "when you see the truth. I expect she's there too."

"Where?" I ask. "And do you mean Grandma Orla?"

They nod.

"'Nostalgia, Violence, and Regrets,'" Fin says. "That's where you'll find her."

"You're not coming?" I ask.

"You deserve to make your own judgments, without me there to sway you."

But I can tell there's something they're not saying. There's another reason they aren't coming with me.

"You're afraid," I say. "You're afraid to face your own past."

"Of course I am," they snap. "I told you what I did to Orla. You are a child. I've existed for centuries. There are many things in the past I cannot bear to repeat."

"They're just memories, Fin. They can't hurt you." I say the words with confidence I don't have. I might just be a kid, but I also know that not facing truths of the past can usually do more harm than good.

"You know not of which you speak," Fin growls. And for a moment, I'm afraid of them. This must show on my face because they soften immediately, the fire disappearing from their shining black eyes. "I'm sorry, Bernadette, I—" They break off. "I cannot face it."

But then they take my hand in theirs and look me straight in the eyes.

"Remember who you are," Fin says. "If you get lost in someone else's memory, remember who you are. If a corrupted memory takes hold of you, remember who you are."

"Corrupted memory?" I squeak, but they just squeeze my hand tighter.

"Just remember who you are," they insist. "That's what brought you to this dimension in the first place. And it's what will see you through any challenge you might find . . . up there."

"I'll stand guard," Fin adds, releasing my hand. "And divert any Confusions who might try to lend a helping tentacle."

"Where are 'Nostalgia, Violence, and Regrets'?" I ask.

"Follow the signs." Fin gestures to a plaque on the wall that was incomprehensible scribbles only a moment before. But in front of my eyes, it changes to English. Detailing the levels of the Memorabilia, with arrows pointing to various ramps. And there, at the very top: Nostalgia, Violence, and Regrets (for Mature Audiences Only): Outer Ramp, all the way to the top.

"Wait, should I leave Mars and Clío with you? Do cats have regrets?"

"Mars can and will make his own choices," Fin says. "And he has. Cats always do."

I turn and see Mars trotting up the ramp ahead of me. He turns, mewing impatiently.

"Clío?" I ask. And I swear she rolls her eyes. Of course she's coming. I doubt I could get her to stay with Fin if I bribed her with the best treats in the world.

"Well, I guess I'm not doing this alone after all," I murmur as I start up the glassy ramp with my kitten and my dog.

"Remember who you are," Fin calls after me as I round the first bend and see a wall of translucent orbs labeled Pets & Pet-Like Animals. I pause; the bubble compass in my chest is back. And it's pulling me toward the shelf.

My hand reaches out before I even register the impulse. A swirl of purple wraps around my hand and I feel a light slap. Did a Dismember just whap my hand away from this memory? Well, now I have to see it. I glance around. If it was a Dismember, it seems to be gone. Mars stands about ten feet farther up the ramp, tail swishing impatiently. Clío is right beside me, her brown eyes locked on the memory my hand hovers over. She's curious too.

I wonder what I need to do to see the memory. Is there some sort of memory video player section, like in libraries with the ancient videotapes from the twentieth century? The question is answered for me the second my hand touches the orb. Which is definitely not glass. Like everything else here, it squishes. There's a split second where I register the spongelike texture before the memory consumes every single one of my senses.

CHAPTER THIRTY-TWO
a popular memory

Maeve's face is pressed to the window of our old green Subaru. Except it's not old. The cloth seats are brand-new. The whole car is brand-new. And Maeve is only six or so, which means I must be barely three. I turn, and there I am. A chubby, red-haired toddler in my car seat. Mom and Dad are in the front, complaining about gawking tourists holding up traffic. But Maeve and I don't care. We could stay here all day. There's a huge bighorn sheep right outside her window.

"Look at the horns!" Maeve cries. She taps on the glass, trying to get the sheep's attention. It doesn't work. "Ber, look at the horns! They make a whole circle! Look!"

And I do look. Both tiny, toddler Ber, and whatever self exists watching the memory. The sheep just blinks its black eyes and continues to lick the salt at the side of the road. Completely unbothered by Maeve's screams of delight.

There's a strange, dissonant chime and the memory wobbles.

"Daily viewing limit reached," a voice says. "Please reshelve memories where you found them. If you cannot remember where you found them, please return to the collections desk so they can be properly shelved."

I blink and I'm back on the ramp in the Memorabilia. The squishy orb rests in my hand, but the disembodied voice continues to ring in my ears.

"If you encountered an unexpected problem with a memory, please inform a curator. Please note: This is a popular memory, please limit viewings to one per visit, so it can be enjoyed by many visitors without degeneration." Then the voice starts over from the beginning. "Daily viewing limit reached. Please reshelve—"

I shove the memory back on the shelf and the voice stops. When I pull my hand back, it's shaking. That was *my* memory. Why did I choose to give it up? *When* did I choose to give it up? And why is it so popular? Nothing happens. It's just my family in our car in Glacier National Park. Sure, that was a particularly huge bighorn sheep. Not that I remember it. Though I do, sort of. Now.

It's like stepping inside the memory again unlocked that day in my brain. Even though I was only three. We met up with the Kalispell Coven later that day. They were only five witches back then. Lindley's parents, another couple, and a woman with black hair I can't remember. Lindley was the only kid. Is that why I was drawn to this memory?

And why is it so popular?

Maybe because Maeve and I were so little. I think of what Fin said about baby blood witches coming here with Mysteries. Because they are cute and entertaining.

Mars meows. He's right. I need to stay focused. I can't let myself get distracted by my own memories.

The Pets & Pet-Like Animals section seems to stretch forever. As I walk past a curving wall of memories, one floats from the shelf. But when I look again, a sunshine-yellow tentacle is grasping the orb. As soon as my eyes focus on it, the tentacle becomes a blur of vague yellow. How many demons are in this place with me?

As I continue up the ramp, I start to notice how many smudges of color and light become hands and tentacles and even mouths when I look at them out of the corner of my eye. I hurry up, glancing down at Clío, who's walking even closer to me, her little paws trotting along, head turning, on high alert.

I'm higher up in the Memorabilia now, but nowhere

near the top. This place feels endless. The next sign I come to reads Friendship, Romance & Love, and I'm fairly certain I won't find any of my own memories here. I've never really had many close friends before this year. I've had acquaintances, kids I'm friendly with at school. But keeping our magic secret has always been a priority, so I never had birthday parties or friends coming over to hang out at our house. Well, other than some of the other blood witches, but hardly any of them are my age.

I expect to pass by this section without feeling any kind of pull toward any particular memory, but after only a few steps, my whole heart basically jumps from my chest toward an orb that glows purple on a shelf high above me. I reach up before I can think better of it or a Dismember can try to stop me. The second my hand touches the orb, I'm transported into the memory.

Mom's full face smiles at me. She's got bright red lipstick on, and her cheeks are flushed. Her hair is shorter than I've ever seen it, cut into a shaggy bob. She's wearing a red dress, a deeper red than her lipstick, and she's dancing.

I step back and see Dad dancing with her. I can tell this is his memory from the way Mom glows. She's perfect. Everyone else blurs and it's like a movie, when they use some sort of camera trick or editing to make sure you know who you're supposed to be looking at, who the main character is. And it's Mom. She's radiant and laughing and I can feel Dad's love for her. And it's like a thousand tiny fireworks go off inside my chest. It's too much. My eyes burn, my heart is going to explode inside my chest, and even if that doesn't matter in this dimension, I'm pretty sure I'm going to need my heart in one piece when I get home.

"Out," I whisper. "Stop. Pause. End memory."

The memory freezes and I blink. I'm back in the Memorabilia. I shove the orb back onto the shelf, my chest tight.

That was the first moment Dad knew he was in love with Mom. She's told me about it. At her cousin's wedding. But I'm so confused. Why would Dad let that memory go? Why would he give it to a Dismember?

And then it clicks. He trusted her to tell him about it. To remind him. They hold the memory together. Her half was enough. And whatever I feel for Cai is peanuts compared with that. The thought makes me sad at first, but then kind of oddly hopeful in a strange way. There's a whole lot I haven't experienced yet. I stare at the shelves of memories. And suddenly I think I get it. Why it's sad to lose one memory, but not a tragedy, especially not when you have people to share them with. Why blood witches would have agreed to share these memories with demons to begin with.

And that's when I hear a sound I've only heard once before in my entire life. The day Grandma Dot died. A sound so seared into my memory I don't think the most powerful Dismember could take it.

It's Grandma Orla. And she's sobbing.

CHAPTER THIRTY-THREE
finding faults

I sprint up the ramp as fast as I can go. I've never been more grateful that I don't get tired or have to worry about lows in this dimension. Grandma Orla's sobs are getting louder, and I hear another voice now, Patrick, I think. But I can't make out what he's saying.

I glance down to make sure Mars and Clío are still with me. They are. I breathe a sigh of relief and round the corner, certain I'm going to find Grandma Orla just around the bend. Instead, I crash straight into a wall of memories.

I'm so sorry. So deeply sorry. I'm not sure what for, but I'd learn a hundred new languages to find new ways to apologize. I'm just so sorry.

I hear Grandma Orla. She's still crying. And that's definitely Patrick talking to her. I need to get to them. I'm so close, and yet—

I'm a bride, dressed in white, waiting under an arbor as a dozen guests stare at me, tears and pity in their eyes.

I'm a soldier, a warrior, a fighter. There is blood on my hands that isn't my own.

I'm a young boy leaving my dog behind as I move to a new country. It's too complicated to take her with us. Too much paperwork. My heart is breaking into pieces as I feed her treats. I feed her my heart, a big piece of it. So she knows I wouldn't do this if I had a choice.

I'm trapped in a verse of a song written for a lover who died long ago. So long ago. I haunt myself.

I'm on a ship, a dagger clutched in shaking hands before I snap it in half and throw it into the sea. But then a name I know interrupts me.

"Bernadette!" It touches something in my chest, like the name has hands and they are squeezing my heart. "Bernadette!" There, again. That name. That name that means something. Something important to me.

"Bernadette Crowley, remember who you are."

Yes. My name. I'm Bernadette Crowley. Daughter of Ciara and Aaron. Sister of Maeve. Granddaughter of Orla. I'm made up of the people I love. I'm made of their love and the love I have for them. I'm a witch. And a powerful one. I'm the blood witch that bound a Mystery, a Mystery named Fin. The same Mystery that's calling my name.

I blink, coming back to myself. Remembering who I am and what I'm here to do.

"I thought you said you couldn't, wouldn't—"

"You were right," Fin says. "I can't let regrets, my own or anyone else's, keep me from helping the people I care about."

I raise my eyebrows.

"You, Bernadette. You are the people I care about."

"Oh."

"Bernie?" This time the voice is Grandma Orla's. "Ber, no, I don't want you to see—"

"It's okay, Grandma," I say, pushing myself off the ground and picking my way through the smashed memories. She's sitting on the floor, Dar standing beside her, pawing at her leg. And she's got a whole pile of memories stacked before her.

"Fin told me what happened," I say as I crouch beside

her. "That you came to the demon dimension a toddler and went back home as a little girl."

"But I didn't remember," Grandma Orla says. "I didn't remember any of it. I didn't remember—" Her voice breaks and I know tears would be streaming down her face if we were in the mortal dimension. "I didn't remember my mother," she says. "I thought it was just because I was so young when she died, but it was—" She hiccups. "It was their fault."

She looks up at Fin and there is pure malice in her eyes.

"I didn't understand," Fin says.

"That's rich," Grandma Orla says.

"Orla, please," Fin says. "I've been trying to tell you, trying to show you—"

Grandma Orla hurls a memory at them. They duck just in time, and it smashes on the floor. Lost.

"No, Grandma!" I pull the next memory she grabs from her hands. It's warm and pulls at my heart in a way that tells me it's part of our history, part of our family.

"Please," I say. "Let me see them."

"No, Bernie," Grandma Orla pleads. "There are things in here, pieces of our past—"

"That you'd rather I don't see," I finish for her. She shakes her head, starting to argue, but I press on. "I think I understand why Great-Great-Grandma did it.

But I want to understand. I want to see and know and make my own choices. I don't want to run from our past, from our history. Not anymore."

I expect her to argue. I expect her to put her foot down and tell me I can't. I expect her to quote the Blood Witch Word and remind me I'm not initiated. I wait for her to put me back in my place as the youngest Crowley with the least understanding of how the world works. But she doesn't. She stares at me for a long moment and then she nods.

"Start with this one," she says. And she hands me a glowing, pale blue orb.

CHAPTER THIRTY-FOUR
the first unbinding

There's a little girl who looks like me. She's dressed in a knee-length blue dress and her curly red hair is braided, though most of it is escaping the braid. She must be only three or four and her chubby little arms are freckled. Even more freckled than mine were at that age.

She's running in circles in a forest I recognize, the forest I walked through with Fin when I first arrived in the demon dimension. Her feet are bare and she's laughing so much she can hardly breathe, not that she needs to in this dimension. And she's chasing a demon. A Mystery demon.

Fin.

Great-Great-Grandma Bernadette is chasing Fin's tail. They let her catch it, and she laughs even harder.

As the memory dissolves, I find myself back in the Memorabilia. Grandma Orla holds out another memory, but I shake my head.

"I need to choose," I say. "I need to choose which to watch next."

"Okay," she says, setting the memory down beside the others.

I sit next to her and close my eyes, feeling for the pull from deep inside me. It guides my hand, and I open my eyes and choose another memory.

Great-Great-Grandma Bernadette is a teen now, or maybe early twenties. She's wearing a skirt that reaches almost to the ground and a wool cape around her shoulders. It's blowing in the wind and the wind is fierce and cold. Salt spray splashes her face, and I realize she's on a cliff above a stormy ocean. I recognize these cliffs. I've been there. The Cliffs of Moher in Ireland. This is before she moved the coven across the Atlantic.

She's standing, facing the ocean, dagger in one hand, the other held out. She mutters a spell, but the wind carries the words away before I can hear them. Then she slices her hand. Not just a gentle stab to a finger, but a slice down the outside of her palm, under her pinky. She squeezes her hand as the blood pools, and as a large drop falls on the grass at her feet, a familiar Mystery demon appears beside her.

"Hello again, Bernadette Crowley," Fin says. *"Let's see what magic we might do together, shall we?"*

They hold out a hand and my great-great-grandma places her still-bleeding hand in it and they shake. Smiles breaking across both of their faces.

When I emerge from the memory, I immediately grab another, letting it show me Great-Great-Grandma Bernadette and Fin's adventures. I see them visiting places I know, others I don't. I'm pretty sure they play a prank on someone who looks like Charlie Chaplin at one point.

Then I see Great-Great-Grandma Ber on a ship alone, staring across the waves as she leaves Ireland behind. And I feel her heart break. I feel the piece of her she leaves behind as she watches until the island disappears from view.

I barely pause as I choose the next memory. And somehow, I know what this one will be before it even pulls me into its pearlescent white glow.

"She'll only be gone a moment," Fin says. *"Just as you were, all those years ago."*

A little girl stands between them in a green dress, her dark brown hair in two braids that hang down over her shoulders. A tiny, adorable Grandma Orla, way before she was a grandma, or a mom. Just barely a toddler.

She holds the hand of a woman who looks so much like Maeve it takes my breath away. She looks barely older than my sister is now.

She crouches down and faces tiny Orla, taking her face in her hands.

"You are going to have so much fun, my love," Great-Grandma Niamh says. "I'll miss you, even though you'll hardly be gone a moment, just like Finny says."

"I will not stand for such nonsense nicknames," Fin says, crossing their arms over their chest indignantly.

"Of course you will," Great-Great-Grandma Ber says. "And more besides, whatever our little Orla comes up with."

"Well, perhaps you are not entirely incorrect in that assessment," Fin says. "Now, Orla? Are you ready to see the demon dimension?"

Great-Grandma Niamh hugs her daughter one more time, and then Fin takes her hand, and they step out of the mortal dimension as I fall from the memory.

My heart aches as the memory dissolves, knowing that was the last time Grandma Orla saw her mom. Knowing that her mom never got to hold her hand or hug her or kiss her face again.

I reach for the next memory, but Grandma Orla pulls it away.

"Not that one, Bernie," she says. "I know you want

to see, need to see as much of this as you can. But this one is only mine."

I want to argue, but instead I reach for the next memory. The last memory. It pulses a deep red and I can feel that it's been calling to me most. My hand trembles as I reach for it and I glance to Fin, who looks like they want to stop me, but they don't. I know what's waiting for me in this memory, but I take it in my hand anyway and let it pull me into the worst moment of my great-great-grandmother's life.

Great-Great-Grandma Bernadette stares through me. She looks like the pictures I've seen of her. She's got my same stubborn chin. But her hair is starting to gray; her face is thinner than it was in her youth. Her eyes sparkle, and I can't figure out the expression on her face because it's dark and the streetlights below cast strange shadows. But she looks impatient, possibly even desperate as she hugs her gray coat around her and stares up at the moon.

She's standing on the rooftop of a building in a city, and when I look beyond her, I see the Empire State Building in the distance. This is Brooklyn. It must be the 1950s, before she moved west.

The air shimmers before her and I see Fin and a little girl step into the mortal dimension. The little girl is clearly Orla, and she's a mess. Her hair is a rat's nest and she still wears the tiny dress she had on when she left the mortal dimension even though she's clearly outgrown it.

The second they appear, Fin beaming and mid-laugh, Great-Great-Grandma launches herself across the space between them and wrenches Orla from Fin's grasp.

"How dare you?" she screams, dropping to her knees and examining her granddaughter. Tears stream down her face as she takes in Orla's dirty face and messy hair.

As her grandmother pulls at her hair and clothes, Orla's smile dissolves and she starts to cry. It's hard to tell how old she is, especially in her messy state.

"I thought you said time wouldn't pass," Great-Great-Grandma Bernadette screams. "It's been years, Finley. What happened?"

"I'm sorry," a small voice says. It's Grandma Orla. "I'm sorry, please don't be mad at Fin, we went on an adventure."

"What is she talking about?" Great-Great-Grandma Bernadette snaps.

"Bernadette, please," Fin says. "You're overreacting. I see that time passed here, and now that I look closer, yes, she's grown a bit. But we had the most marvelous opportunity to—"

"Where did you take her?" Great-Great-Grandma Ber growls.

"Somewhere wonderful," Orla answers, brightening

for a moment before beginning to cry again when she sees the fear on her grandma's face.

Great-Great-Grandma Bernadette hugs Orla to her tightly for a long minute before she puts her hands over her ears and glares up at Fin.

"Niamh died," *she hisses so quietly I almost don't hear it. And I wish I didn't. I don't want to. I don't want to see this part. Fin already told me, and I don't want to see it myself. To feel it myself. But I'm not running away from this. I said I wanted to know the truth of my family, and that means knowing the truth of Fin too.*

"No," Fin cries. "Oh, no, Bernadette. I'm so s—"

"Don't you dare say you're sorry," Great-Great-Grandma Bernadette yells.

Orla howls, tears streaming down her face as she clings to her grandmother.

"This is over," Great-Great-Grandma Bernadette spits at Fin. "We are over."

"Bernadette, please—"

"I unbind you, Finley MacIntire," she says. "Now and forever. Blood witches will never treat with Mysteries again."

Fin's expression goes cold as the moonlight.

"You don't mean that," they say.

"I most certainly do," she growls.

"You'll regret this," Fin snaps. "And your magic will

weaken. We are the source of your true power; without Mysteries you'll only have lower-order demons for chores and party tricks. You will have no true magic."

"We'll find a way," Great-Great-Grandma Bernadette says, standing straight and pushing Orla behind her. "You will stay away from my family forever. I will make sure of it."

"You will disrupt the balance," Fin says.

"I don't care about the balance," she shrieks. "I care about my family."

"And am I not your family too?" Fin asks, a tremor in their voice.

"Not anymore." Tears stream down my great-great-grandma's face and her voice shakes as she pulls out her dagger and starts a spell.

Our partnership is at an end,
From this dimension, I now send,
Finley released from solemn vow,
Bernadette unbinds you now.

She slices her hand again, deeper, but along the same side of her palm she cut all those years ago when she stood on the Cliffs of Moher and bound Fin to her for the first time. As the blood seeps from her hand, Fin starts to flicker, just as they did when I unbound them.

"You don't want to do this," Fin says. "You'll change your mind."

"Not if I forget you," Great-Great-Grandma Bernadette says. "Not if every blood witch who lives in this dimension forgets all about our bargain with the Mysteries and only learns of your treachery from this day forward."

"Try it, then," Fin snaps as they continue to flicker. "But without my power you won't be anything. Blood witches are nothing without Mysteries."

"And family is nothing without trust," Great-Great-Grandma Bernadette says. Her voice is so quiet.

"I love you, Finny," a small voice says from behind her, just as Fin disappears from the mortal dimension.

CHAPTER THIRTY-FIVE
the start of something new

I emerge from the memory with my heart aching and absolute chaos raging around me. Fin and Grandma Orla stand over me on either side while Clío stands in my lap, growling at a woman it takes me a moment to recognize.

Lindley, the head witch of the Kalispell Coven and attempted murderer of Komorebi and my sister, is just as blond and skinny and short as I remember. Her high-necked white shirt is torn, and her scowl is nasty as she takes a memory orb from the shelf beside her and hurls it at the ground.

"Stop, Lindley," a young witch I don't recognize yells. He's a young man in a tattered blue sweater. He has fair skin and brown hair, and his glasses are definitely not supposed to be as bent and crooked as they are.

He whimpers as whatever memory Lindley has hurled at his feet envelops him.

"She's out of control," a tall woman with curly hair says. "She insisted we come up here, said it was the only way to find the truth of the Crowley power. But all we've seen is anguish and heartache. The voice said to only watch one of these memories. She's watched at least two dozen."

A vortex of purple and red swirls around Lindley. It's a bunch of Dismembers, grabbing at her hair and clothes, but she swats them away.

"We just have to find the right memory," Lindley sneers. "The secrets of the Crowley power were lost generations ago, but I know they're here."

"You're right," I say, pushing Clío gently out of my lap and climbing to my feet, careful not to nudge any of the other memories.

"Bernadette," Grandma Orla growls in warning.

"No," I say. "No more secrets. Not about this. Lindley, you're right," I repeat. And her jaw drops open in shock before she smiles a wicked smile. "But you're also wrong," I add quickly. "There's no spell hiding Crowley power here. Just memories. And Mysteries."

Lindley's smile disappears and she snarls as she grabs at her hair. "No more Crowley riddles!" she screams.

"The Mysteries aren't a riddle," I say. "They're the answer."

"Of course you would say that," Lindley spits.

"She's right," Patrick adds. He stands beside Grandma Orla, a hand resting on her shoulder. "The Crowleys are secretive for many reasons, but the Mysteries are the answer, just as I've always suspected."

"We're facing the truth," I add, stepping a tiny bit closer to Lindley. "And you need to do the same."

"I'm not taking orders from some—"

"There they are," a voice shouts. An eerie, multi-voiced voice that I immediately recognize at the three-headed Mystery who flew away with Grandma Orla. "Sneaky little witches, giving us the slip. But mortals always find their way here. Inevitable as the Mysteries."

"It's always the Memorabilia," Margaret says. A few of the Kalispell Coven witches throw their hands over their ears at her screeching voice.

"Oh, and the boring loud ones are here too," Cadwalader says. "Well, that's unfortunate."

"We're quite done with them, don't you think?" Margaret asks.

Lindley shouts a protest, but the Mysteries ignore her.

"Right this way," Cadwalader says, gesturing with both their dragon-like arms and wings toward a glowing ripple in the air.

"Wait, no, no!" Lindley cries. They ignore her. She reaches for another memory, but Margaret stretches out a death-pale hand that definitely has claws on the end and plucks it from her grasp, setting it back on the shelf and shoving Lindley back into the mortal dimension.

The rest of her coven follows without protest. They seem eager to get back to the world they came from. They look distressed, their clothes torn and hair messy. I remember someone saying something about Chaos Canyon. I hope they're not too traumatized. Well, maybe I hope they're a little traumatized. Enough that they stop sacrificing animals for their twisted blood magic.

The last of the coven stops before the portal, and when they turn, I see it's Devon, Lindley's husband. His hands are on his stomach, where a large, dark red stain blooms on his shirt. And I suddenly remember how Lindley kept the Tairseach open. She stabbed him.

"Can—" he starts, his voice gruff as if he hasn't used it in days. "Can I stay?" he finishes. "It's just . . . well, I'm not sure I'll survive back in the mortal dimension."

"You might if I come with you," Cadwalader says, their voices eerie and menacing.

"Cadwalader . . ." Margaret says. "Remember what happened the last time you were in the mortal dimension."

All three of Cadwalader's mouths smirk while all five of their eyes narrow.

"Indeed, I do," they say. "But yes, I'll keep it, sorry, him. At least for now."

"'For now' is fine," Devon says quickly, releasing his

hands from his stomach. The wound there is gruesome, but like all other bodily functions, it seems to be in some sort of stasis in this dimension.

"And these?" Margaret says, turning to look at my family and Patrick, who's been standing silently beside Grandma Orla, a hand on her shoulder.

"I'll take care of them," Fin says. And just an hour ago, I might have thought it was a threat, but now I hear it for the promise it is.

"If you say so," Margaret says, and they wave a clawed hand and the shimmering portal disappears.

"It's that simple?" I ask Fin. "You could have just sent me home? You could have just sent Grandma Orla home?"

"Sending humans back to your home dimension is quite easy, yes," Fin says. "Us following you there after what your namesake did is quite different and altogether difficult." They stoop to look me directly in the eyes. "But it would have been very hard indeed to *just* send you home," they say.

"Bernie, we can't trust—" Grandma Orla starts, but I turn to her, crossing my arms over my chest.

"Yes," I say. "We can. I can. I know what Fin did was wrong, so wrong, but—okay, I'm going to sound totally cheesy saying this, but two wrongs don't make a right."

"That saying has nothing to do with cheese," Fin mutters, but falls silent when I glare at them.

"I understand why your grandma did what she did," I say, crossing to Grandma Orla. "But I think it might have been a tiny bit of an overreaction."

"You'll understand better when you're a mother someday," Grandma Orla says, lifting her chin defiantly.

"Orla—" Patrick begins, but I can't let him fight this battle for me. It's time that Grandma Orla listened, really listened.

"I might," I admit. "But I also understand *now*. I understand Fin made a mistake, and I understand our family broke a promise. Great-Great-Grandma Ber made a decision for every blood witch in the world that wasn't hers to make."

"It was ours to make," Grandma Orla insists. "The Crowleys—"

"No, Grandma. It wasn't. No one should make that big of a decision for everyone else. We need to make amends. We need to stop running and hiding from our secrets and our past."

"But my own mother, Bernie—I missed my own— You stole—" She turns to Fin, blinking nonexistent tears away furiously.

"I want to choose forgiveness," I say. "For us. For our family. I understand what secrecy gave Great-Great-Grandma, but it doesn't give us that. It doesn't give me that. I want to take risks; I have to."

Grandma Orla's lip quivers, but after a long time, she nods. And the relief that crashes through me is like a tidal wave. I throw myself into her arms and she hugs me tight for a long, long time.

"I think it's time to return to the mortal dimension," Patrick says. "If you would be so kind, Margaret?"

"Kindness has nothing to do with it," they say, but they wave their unnaturally long arms again and the air begins to shimmer.

"Wait!" I cry.

The Mystery turns to me, their face still hidden by their floor-length curtain of black hair.

"If Devon could stay," I ask, my voice shaking. "Well, if Devon could stay, could I? Could I stay in this dimension with the Mysteries and be . . . not a diabetic?"

"Bernie, no!" Grandma Orla cries, but I turn to Fin.

It's an idea that has been growing in my mind since the Expanse. An idea that fully took root when Fin told me about blood witch babies spending time here. After I got over my shock. Because I'm not a diabetic here. No blood sugar. No injections. No lows. No highs. And even with all the stress of finding Grandma Orla, of going through the Squelch and learning my family's secrets, my brain has felt so free.

"You could," Fin says. They're standing beside me, looking down. I can't read the expression in their eyes, and I realize mine are filled with tears. Which should be impossible. But so much about everything in my life since I met them should be impossible. "You could stay here, for a time at least."

"I could?"

Grandma Orla makes a strangled sound, but I hold Fin's gaze.

"It would be strange, and not without struggle," they say.

"And I wouldn't be a diabetic?"

"Not in any real sense, no. Not until you returned to the mortal dimension. Whenever you chose to do so."

I pull out my insulin pump. The white swirl of pixels is still there. It's just a box here. A box filled with the precious liquid that I live or die by back in my dimension. And for a second, I let myself really think about it. About leaving my life behind. About going on adventures through the Mystery dimension with Fin, never having to think about insulin-to-carb ratios, hypoglycemia, or my period. My body has felt like a battleground for as long as I can remember.

Too big.

Too squishy.

Too much blood sugar.

Not enough blood sugar.

Too sweaty.

Too loud.

Too much.

Not enough.

Maybe if I stayed, I could be free of all of that long enough to figure out who I am.

"I don't know what to do." My voice breaks. "Tell me what I should do."

"I can't make that decision for you," Fin says. "But I can tell you what I believe about you. What I believe you are capable of, should you choose to return to your dimension."

I nod.

"You, Bernadette Crowley, can be the start of something new that faces the truth of the old. You can be a bridge. A metaphor. Carrying meaning far beyond yourself. You can't change your family's past, but you can be an important part of its future."

"But what if I just want to be a witch?" I ask.

"That's perfectly fine too." Fin's eyes shine as they take my hand. I know they know I've decided. "Sometimes the world will assign meanings for you. And it will be your choice whether you step into them willingly or are dragged. You are not going to lead a small life, Bernadette. You are quite like your namesake in that way."

And it feels like I'm back in the ruined shack on Shelter

Island, watching Fin be ripped away from me again. But this time, I'm the one who's choosing to leave.

Doubt fills my mind, but certainty clears my heart. This isn't about choosing between Fin and Grandma Orla, between a world where I'm a diabetic and one where I'm not. It's about trusting myself, knowing there is no one right decision. There are always going to be people and things pulling me in different directions. But I'm the one who needs to live with my decisions. I might have regrets, but I want to live a full enough life to earn them. And there's only one place I can do that.

I decide to trust myself most of all.

"I'm going home," I say. And I hear Grandma Orla's cry of relief.

"The brave choice," Fin says. And then a wolfish grin splits their face. "Would you like me to come with you?"

CHAPTER THIRTY-SIX
mixing magics

"You're coming?" I squeal. Like, actually squeal, like a little piglet. "You can come back to the mortal dimension with us?"

"I can," Fin says. "And I will, but only with your grandmother's permission."

My heart freezes as I stare between Fin and Grandma Orla. I want to beg; I want to plead. But I know I need to let her make her decision. I need to let her change her mind.

"If I agree to this," she begins. "If," she repeats, louder, "you are bound to me, not to Ber. Not yet. She needs time to sort through her increasingly complicated life, and you and I have some catching up to do."

"That we do, Orla," Fin says. "That we most certainly do."

"Can you still smell my blood sugar?" I ask. "If you're bound to Grandma Orla?"

"I suppose that depends on the spell we use for the binding," Fin says.

I finally let the "please" that had been building up in my chest tumble out of my mouth and Grandma Orla laughs, she actually laughs. And I'd forgotten that it's basically my favorite sound in the whole entire world.

"Okay, Finny," she says. "Let's craft this spell."

Grandma Orla and Fin put their heads together to create a spell that will bind them to her but allow their purpose in the mortal dimension to extend to blood sugar sniffing. I don't know when Margaret and Cadwalader left, but they're gone, and so is Devon. And for a moment, my heart stops when I can't find Mars. But then I hear a mew and find him stuck on the highest shelf of memories, Clío stationed below him, keeping guard.

"You two have been very brave," I say, trying to get Mars to jump down into my arms. He refuses. But a moment later Fin scoops him off the shelf and deposits him back on my shoulder.

"Are you ready to go home?" Fin asks.

I nod, reaching down and scratching Clío's soft ears, thinking of how happy she'll be to see Cai and Mom and Dad. And even Phoebe.

Which makes me realize how happy I'll be to see them all too. It was tempting, to stay here, to choose an easier but lonelier path. But Fin's right, I have big things to do in my dimension. I can feel it. And my new friends and their magics are going to be a part of that. I might just not spring that part of my slowly forming plan for the entire transformation of blood witch society on Grandma Orla for a little while. She's been through a lot. I understand now that she was afraid of other magics, afraid of Mysteries. But one family's fear doesn't justify how we treat other magical people. I think she's starting to see that, and I'm glad I'll be there to help her.

"After you," Fin says, and I look over to see Patrick helping Grandma Orla through the shimmering portal.

"No," I say. "With you." I hold out my hand, and they take it. Their fur is warm and soft, and they hold gently but firmly as we usher Clío through the portal and follow quickly behind her.

The feeling of being stretched in every direction at once returns, but passes more quickly when going from demon to mortal dimension. But the second my feet land on solid ground, my body feels like it weighs a million pounds. I'm exhausted, my mouth is dry. My period is *definitely* back. And all my pump alarms seem to be going off at the same time.

"Ber, is that you?" Mom's voice calls. It's dark, and as I look around, I see we're not in Grandma Orla's garden, like I expected us to be. We're not even in our backyard.

"Where are we?" I ask as I squint into the darkness, my eyes absolutely not adjusting. It's cold, really cold. And there's not even a sliver of moon in the sky.

Then I see the candles. Hundreds of them, spread around the ground in a huge circle. A circle we're standing right in the middle of.

"Ber!" This time it's Cai who says my name, and the next thing I know I'm basically tackled by my boyfriend.

"Cai! What are you doing here?"

I feel a nudge against my leg, and look down to see Clío, eagerly waiting for me to hold out my hand. She seems relieved as I put out a hand and she bumps her nose into my palm. I'm low. Well, guess I'm a diabetic again.

"I've got a juice box," Maeve's voice says, and she appears out of the darkness beside me. "Or gummies."

"I'll take the gummies," I say. It'll be nice to chew something after not needing to eat for— "How long were we gone?" I ask.

"How long did it feel like to you?" Cai asks.

"It's hard to explain," I say through my second mouthful of gummies. And part of me already feels like the Mystery dimension was a dream.

"Wait, what's going on?" I ask as my eyes start to fully adjust to the flickering candlelight. "Why are you all here? And where is here?"

"We're on the top of Blue Mountain," Maeve explains. "Away from any geenin Halloween nonsense. Tonight is Samhain."

A week! We were gone a whole week.

"Cai and Phoebe thought it might be our best chance to bring you back," Mom says. And it's so good to see her, I feel like I might cry. And then I realize I am crying. Maybe I have been since we got back to this dimension. "We were going to open another Tairseach, carefully, and with a lot of help. But it seems you didn't need us to after all." Mom pulls me into the best hug of my entire life.

"Us?" I ask, pulling away and looking around. And when I do, I see way more than just the Bitterroot Coven. There are dozens of witches here. No, not just witches. Mages too.

"Cai was insistent we work together," Mom says. "And no, he didn't use his mind magic, just some really good debate tactics."

"You worked together?" I ask. "The different covens?"

"I mean, we were trying," Phoebe says. "But then you just showed up before we could even conjure the big scary demon." She sounds a bit disappointed.

"So, we can all just go home, then?" a voice I don't recognize calls.

A murmur goes through the crowd, and I have a really wild idea. Maybe because I'm low, maybe because I've just returned from another dimension. Maybe just because.

"Wait, please," I call. "Can everyone just wait a second?"

"Pipe down and listen to Ber," Maeve shouts, and everyone falls silent.

My hands start to sweat, and I shove the last few gummies into my mouth, chewing quickly. Everyone's staring. Which is what I wanted. But I may have let the low blood sugar impulsivity get the better of me.

"Um, I just wanted—" I falter. Cai steps up beside me, slipping his hand into mine. And it's only then I realize Fin is nowhere to be seen. I panic, looking around into the darkness, searching.

"Don't worry, little witch," Fin's voice says, right next to my ear. Startling me so much I almost jump out of my skin. "I'm staying hidden for now, but I'm here."

"Oh," Cai says, his eyes going wide.

"Yeah," I whisper to him. "I'll explain later. For now, could you just . . . you know, do your thing?"

"Are you sure you want me to?" he asks. "I don't think you actually need me—"

"I do," I say quickly. "I want you to, and I need you. I'm really glad you're my boyfriend."

"Dang, I think that's the first time you've used that word out loud," he says. "I like it. Though, about that—" He breaks off, an expression flitting across his face that I can't quite place. "Don't worry," he adds quickly. "Not about you. Or us. And it can wait. I'm just glad to have you back in this dimension." He leans forward and kisses me on the cheek. As his lips touch my skin, all my worries and doubts disappear. And I don't even feel embarrassed as someone wolf-whistles and I remember everyone is watching us, waiting for me to speak.

"Thank you," I start. "That's the main thing I wanted to say. Want to say. I really am so grateful. I know what it cost you to work together. And you did that for me, and that's not a small thing. And I won't ever forget it." I pause, taking a deep breath. The sensation of the cool night air entering my lungs grounds me.

"I know I'm just a kid. But I just got back from a whole different dimension, and I learned some really important lessons there. And I had help getting there.

Really important help from some really important people."

A murmur goes through the crowd, but everyone falls silent. Waiting for me to speak. It's surreal. I'd never have thought this possible in a million years or a thousand dimensions. Samhain—the most powerful night of the year. And here we all are, blood witches, weather witches, mind mages, and plant mages. Together, as if we're all one coven.

And everyone is listening to me. They care what I have to say. At least for now.

It's almost enough to chase all my thoughts right out of my head, but Cai puts a hand on my shoulder and squeezes. Not taking anything from me. Just reminding me of my own strength.

"Patrick Walsh didn't exactly choose to visit, but he absolutely chose to help me. He didn't have to. He didn't have to use the same knowledge and skills my own family mocked him for to help me, but he did." I turn to him. "I'm sorry. And thank you. Go raibh míle maith agat," I add in Irish. He smiles and nods. Then he and Grandma Orla share a look I can't read. But I guess they have lots of things to work out between them. We all do.

"Most of all, I couldn't have done any of this without Cai and Phoebe. My friends. And brilliant mages."

My throat gets tight as Phoebe smiles, and I feel Cai's hand tighten on my shoulder. "They were patient with me when I didn't understand the ignorance that came with blood witch secrecy, and they trusted me to try new spells and mix our magics in new ways. Heck, they were ready to follow me into the demon dimension."

"Yeah, honestly still a little bummed that part didn't work," Phoebe says.

"There's always next time," Cai says.

"Oh, absolutely not," Mom says. And I can feel my little impromptu speech going entirely off the rails. I need to wrap this up.

"Anyway, thank you. I'm glad I'm home. Back where I belong. With all of you. And with my family. I know we aren't always the easiest family to get along with . . ."

Patrick Walsh laughs louder than anyone and Grandma Orla swats at him.

"Understatement of the century," someone quips.

"But we're going to do better," I say. "We have a lot to learn from each other. It's time for blood witches to share our secrets. Not all of them," I add quickly at the look on Grandma Orla's face. "But some."

And even with the adrenaline of the moment, my eyelids are heavy. I'm tired, so tired. The aftereffects of my low and the whole adventure through another dimension are catching up with me.

"I think it's time to get this witch to bed," Mom says, crossing to me and pulling me into a side hug. The second I relax into her full waist, I feel just how deep my exhaustion goes and I almost fall asleep on my feet.

People say their goodbyes and I promise Cai I'll text him first thing in the morning. Phoebe waves as her great-grandma bustles her away.

Mom practically carries me over to the Direct Dad conjures, which deposits us in the backyard.

Grandma Orla stares up at her house as we turn to go inside.

"Your demons are all gone," I say. "And Patrick ate your Hobnobs."

"I'll replace them," Patrick says, taking Grandma Orla by the arm.

"Wait," I say as they start to walk toward her house. "What about your magic? You sacrificed your magic to open the Tairseach. Did you find it again? In the demon dimension?"

"In a way," Grandma Orla says. And she looks to my left, where I see Fin for just a moment. Long enough for them to wink.

"Come on, Ber," Dad calls from the porch. "I'll refill your pump and get you a new sensor."

"Thanks," I call after him. "Coming!" I run over to Grandma Orla and give her one more hug.

"Thank you," I whisper into her shoulder.

"I love you, Bernie," she whispers back into my hair. "Now get in there and get your fancy insulin pump sorted out. You can show me how it works tomorrow."

"Deal," I say, and hurry to join Mom, Dad, and Maeve in the kitchen.

My legs are shaky as I collapse onto a stool. But when I hold out my hand, Clío doesn't alert. I'm not low anymore at least.

"Are you still here?" I whisper as Mom and Dad argue over whether all the bubbles are out of the insulin syringe before refilling the cartridge.

"Indeed, I am, little witch," Fin whispers. "And you're at 173."

"Thanks," I whisper back.

A few minutes later Mom sends me upstairs, and Maeve hovers over me as I brush my teeth and put in a new sensor. She reminds me to change my pad and helps me when it gets fully stuck to my hands as I try to stick it into my pajama shorts.

"We're going to get you some period panties, stat," she says.

I'm too tired to even grumble a reply.

It feels like forever before I finally collapse into bed, and I don't have the energy to pull my duvet up and over me. But someone does it for me.

Maeve.

"Okay, but please, just tell me one thing about the demon dimension," she says.

"Imtootiredicanttalk," I mutter in a single word, already half asleep.

"Come on, Ber, tell me something. Anything. I'm dying."

"Tomorrow," I mumble. "Or next week. Once I've slept for at least—" But then I break off. And I must be deliriously tired, because I giggle as a thought occurs to me. It's absurd. Ridiculous. But it's also too perfect.

"What?" my sister demands, her long hair falling into her face as she leans forward.

"You know what, Maeve?" I whisper, snuggling into my pillows and letting Clío, Mars, Frangi, and Dar all squish in beside me. She leans in even closer, until her ear is just inches away from my mouth.

"I'm not at liberty to say."

And I fall asleep to the cobblestone sound of Fin's laughter.

EPILOGUE
Winter Solstice

It's strangely warm for solstice, but I'm not complaining, especially since Grandma Orla and Fin insisted this type of magic needs to be done outside. In the weeks since we got back to the mortal dimension, life has been . . . well, just as weird as always. But it's settling into a new kind of weird. And kind of wonderful.

Fin has revealed themself to the whole family. Mom refuses to let them come to school with me since I have Clío and my CGM, but sometimes they sneak in anyway. Not to cheat. (Okay, maybe to *help*. Just a little.) They also started scheming with Grandma Orla and that's what got us all here today, in the backyard, on solstice, where I'm going to get to craft my dagger. Grandma Orla and Fin even took a little (authorized) field trip to Ireland to get a piece of hawthorn wood for the handle.

It's unconventional to craft my dagger almost two years before my official initiation, but the Bitterroot Coven has become rather unconventional since Samhain. It helps that Dutch and his family fully up and left. Well, not the valley. They're still living south of Missoula. But they're not part of our coven anymore. Except Drew. Who's here to support me today. Along with seven of his witch kittens in training. Little calico fuzzballs are zooming all around the clearing, even with Cai trying to communicate the vibe.

I don't mind. I want this to be fun. I know it's serious too.

"Okay, we've got the stone of the place your heart calls home," Cai says, holding up the stone I've chosen for the blade of my dagger. It's dark green quartzite I picked out of Flathead Lake on Cai's birthday last month. I've spent hours filing it down to a point. "And we've got 'the wood of a sacred tree at the place of your roots.'" He points to the hawthorn handle Patrick helped me whittle. "But what's 'the jewel that speaks to the truth of your magic'?"

"Fin said they have that part covered," I say.

"Cool," Cai says.

Fin and Grandma Orla have a new theory about

daggers, and I'm the guinea pig. And I'm absolutely psyched. We're bridging the old ways and the new. I'm not exactly leading the way—I'm leaving that to Maeve and Drew and Grandma Orla and people who have a lot more interest in arguing (or as they say, debating) than I do. But we're making progress. Sometimes it's two steps forward before we jump back or fall over or collapse. But I'll take it.

And I was thrilled to get to be the first blood witch to try crafting a truly modern dagger. Besides, Mom said if we didn't do something to harness my power soon, I'd probably start conjuring accidentals again, even with my CGM and Fin and Cai. It seems that it's not only blood witch babies whose magic gets magnified after spending some time in the demon dimension. So I need a tool to help channel my power ASAP. And today is finally the day.

"Ready?" Grandma Orla asks as Mars chases Drew's kittens around her feet, nearly tripping her.

"Was that question for me or the cats?" I ask.

"Everyone!" she cries, throwing up her hands in exasperation. "Everyone get ready! It's Bernie's big moment."

"I'll be inside," Cai says, kissing me on the cheek and handing Clío's leash to Maeve. "Good luck!"

He was allowed to come to the ritual, and to help us prepare. And he'll join us for the Solstice Fire and snacks once I'm done. But Grandma Orla put her foot down, metaphorically and literally, at the idea of Cai actually observing the ritual. He gives a cheery wave and disappears into the house.

"You've got the conjuring down?" Maeve asks.

"I've had it memorized since the day after you helped me finalize it," I say.

"Okay, well, I've got a copy written down, just in case—"

"Thank you," I say. "I'll nod if I need it."

She smiles, pushing one of her braids behind her shoulder as she stands next to me.

I'm kneeling at the northern edge of the circle. Closest to home. To my home. Grandma Orla sits on the east side, closest to Ireland. And the rest of my family, plus Drew and at least ten cats, fills the circle.

I settle the stone and hawthorn handle on a purple cloth before me as Grandma Orla lights a bundle of juniper. As the smoke fills the air, I look to Fin.

"I told you I'd source the jewel," they say. "This is an experiment, something never done before. Well, you can never say never, witch memory is long, and Mystery memory is longer, but—"

"Fin . . ." I remind them. "The jewel?"

"Yes, of course. I offer a piece of myself, as a gesture of loyalty to the family I love."

They raise their hand to their mouth and bite down. A drop of ruby-red blood pools on their fingertip, a striking contrast to their pearly white fur. Then they pluck the drop from their finger, holding it out to me.

I hesitate for just a second. It's not that I'm squeamish about blood at this point, but this is not what I was expecting *at all*.

"Trust me," Fin says.

I nod and open my hand. But instead of blood dripping into it, a small, red jewel lands in my palm.

"It's beautiful," I say, holding it up to the stark winter sunlight.

"I hope it matches your power," Fin says. And then they step back into their position at the southern edge of the circle.

Grandma Orla smiles, setting her bundle of juniper on the ground before her and holding up her hands.

"We gather today to support Bernie, Bernadette Orla Baron Crowley, as she crafts her dagger. With hawthorn, quartzite, and a stone most precious." She looks between me and Fin and her gaze lingers on them as she continues. "Thank you all for witnessing this moment. I'm grateful, and honored."

"As am I," Fin says. "More than you know."

And now it's time to begin.

We decided on a Bridge, though any Mend demon

would have done the trick. But a Bridge felt right, after all Fin's talk about me being a metaphor.

I take the sharpened stone, my breath high in my chest as I prick my ring finger on my left hand. I feel my cheeks heat as I have to stab it a second time, but then there's a nice big drop of blood. My hand shakes as I lower it toward the piece of hawthorn wood, placing the stone beside it.

> What is separate now combine,
> Purposes to be aligned.
> Each with power all its own
> Newly joined, magic honed,
> Take of hawthorn, stone, and gem—
> Leave me what you make of them.

As I say the final syllable, a pale, gray-green Bridge demon bursts into our dimension. Its tentacles reach down, grabbing the pieces and assembling my dagger. They stretch and wrap, until every bit of wood and stone is obscured by shimmering green appendages. And then there's a pop and the Bridge disappears, leaving my dagger behind. Intact. Whole.

I pick it up with trembling hands as everyone waits in silence.

The red blood-drop jewel is askew on the handle. Just ever so slightly off-kilter. And that seems perfect.

"So mote it be," I say.

"So mote it be!" everyone echoes. A cheer goes up, and Maeve tackles me in a hug.

Dad gives me a special holster he's crafted; it's made to go on a strap around my neck.

"I noticed you liked that about Patrick's," he says, ruffling my hair as I hug him tightly.

"Thank you," I say. "Thank you so, so much." I tuck my new dagger into the holster and slip it around my neck.

I start to run into the house to get Cai, but then I see Grandma Orla gazing off into the night, a strange expression on her face.

"You okay, Grandma?" I ask, bumping my shoulder into hers.

"Oh yes, Bernie, of course," she says quickly. "And I'm so proud of you." She smiles, but there's something in her eyes that worries me.

"I know this has all been a lot for you," I say. She waves a hand, but I keep talking. "No, really. I get it now. I won't forget what I saw in the Memorabilia, what your grandma did for you."

Grandma Orla's lip twitches as her jaw tightens.

"It's brave, to let Fin back into our lives for good," I say. "To let other magics into our lives, and the witches and mages who practice them."

"I'm sorry," Grandma Orla says. "I know you saw what happened, but, well, I was afraid. Of other magics, of the things I didn't remember from my childhood. But isn't that what all prejudice is rooted in? Fear?"

"Um, Grandma . . . are you admitting you were prejudiced?" I bring my hand to my chest in feigned shock and start a little when I feel my dagger resting there. My new dagger. The first of its kind.

"I am, Bernie," Grandma Orla says. "And I'm grateful you're patient with me. But you know secrecy is for all our sake too? Not just blood witches."

"I know," I say. "I'm not trying to change the world or anything."

"Don't be so sure of that." Grandma Orla pulls me into a hug. "I think that might be your destiny and burden, my brave girl." She kisses the top my head and then gently pushes me toward the party that's beginning. Dad is prepping the supplies for s'mores while Maeve stokes the fire and Drew tries to keep the kittens from lighting their tails aflame.

"Do you like it?" Fin asks. I jump. I didn't hear them approach. I almost never hear them approach. But I'm not sure I'll ever get used to how stealthy they really are when they want to be.

"I love it," I say, holding up my dagger. *My* dagger.

"That Bridge did a shoddy job with the jewel placement," Fin says.

"No." I shake my head. "It's perfect. Because it's not. Just like me. It's a bit . . ."

"Strange? Askew? Cockeyed? Skewjawed? Hodgepodge?"

"Unique," I say, cutting Fin off. "I was going to say 'unique.'"

"That it is," Fin says. "And that you are."

"So . . ." I trail off, uncertain how to bring up this particular topic that's been on my mind since the demon dimension. "Okay, so babies going to the demon dimension." Well, that was not as subtle as I hoped for. Oh well. "That was an exchange for Mysteries' power in this dimension, right?"

"Of a kind," Fin says.

"So, let's say if someday, I'm not saying today, I just got my dagger and all, but just, someday, if I were to bind you—if you wanted to be bound to me again, instead of Grandma Orla. Would I have to promise you my babies?"

Fin lets out a bark of a laugh, but then goes very silent and serious in an instant, leaning down to whisper what they say next.

"That's exactly what it means," they say. Then they straighten up, a wicked gleam in their eyes.

"But if I don't have kids?" I ask. "Could I not bind you then? Do I have to promise you Maeve's future theoretical offspring or something?"

"You cannot promise anyone else's children on their behalf."

I breathe a sigh of relief. "Well, that's probably good."

"Questions for another day, little witch," Fin says. "But I'm delighted to be in this dimension, bound to a Crowley once more."

An hour later, after the sun has set, Cai and I are sitting on a blanket next to the fire. I've shown him my new dagger and he's explained how sharp it is to Mars and Clío, who are curled up next to us. But now he's been silent for a long time as we watch the flames dance in the firepit. And I see a newly familiar look cross his face.

"The night I came back," I say. "There was something you didn't tell me. I've seen the same look on your face since then, and I haven't wanted to bring it up. I don't want to push you or anything, but you know you can tell me anything, right? It's kind of only fair with the whole mind mage situation."

I nudge my shoulder into his, and he smiles and shakes his head.

"Hey, I've been doing a lot better at—"

"I know," I say. "You have, but really, Cai. What's up?"

He leans forward, grabbing the edge of the blanket we're sitting on and picking at the fraying weave.

"I've been trying to find a way to tell you," he says. "But you were so busy with research and prep." He falls silent.

"Well, I'm done now," I say, staring down at my brand-new dagger hanging against my chest. "So what is it?"

Cai's quiet for a long time and I wait, letting him find the words as we look at the crackling flames.

"So, you know how we think that spending time with Fin's mind has sort of supercharged my magic?" he asks.

"Yeah." It's a theory Fin confirmed when we came back to the mortal dimension. Yet another new mixing of magics we don't fully understand.

"And how it sort of changed my magic—not in a bad way," he adds.

I nod.

"Well, that's not the only thing that changed."

"What do you mean?"

"I'm . . . well." He drops the edge of the blanket and runs a hand through his hair. "So the way Fin experiences gender, or doesn't," he says. "That feels right to me somehow. So, even though I still very much want to be your boyfriend, I'm not sure I'm a boy, exactly. I'm not a girl either. That's kind of—"

"Cai, are you trying to tell me you're nonbinary?"

"I mean, I think I prefer gender nonconforming? Or maybe enby? Or maybe I don't want any labels at all?" They scrunch up their face and it's so adorable I might just explode.

"Then no labels at all," I say.

"Really?" they ask.

"Of course. I don't love you because you're a boy. I love you because you're you."

It takes me a full thirty seconds of Cai staring at me, mouth hanging slightly open, eyes wide, for me to realize I've just fully said I love you.

"So, you love me, huh?" they ask, a smirk spreading across their annoyingly good-looking face.

"And what if I do?" I ask, my heart hammering in my chest.

"Then that would be really cool," they say. "Because I definitely love you, Bernadette Crowley."

And I smile as they lean forward, brush my hair behind my ear, and kiss me.

We only break apart when Maeve shouts at us to "stop embarrassing her." And even then, we sit there, foreheads touching, until Clío shoves between us and demands to be petted.

I sit by the fire with my boyfriend, my family, my Mystery, my dog, our cats. It's a lot. I'm a lot. And I'm still a diabetic. And a blood witch. And it's still complicated. It probably always will be.

But I'm really glad I decided to come back. Even with diabetes. It's worth it. Cai's worth it. My family's worth it. My magic's worth it.

Our life, this life, is worth it.

ACKNOWLEDGMENTS

This book has been a journey. At one point it felt like I might need to go to the demon dimension myself to conjure a conclusion that felt worthy of the story. I finally feel like I found it, with a lot of help. I hope you agree, and if you don't, please just feed that memory to a Dismember before we talk.

Here's my attempt to say thank you, insufficient as it will be, to the people who helped me do justice to Ber and Fin and complicated family histories.

First and foremost, to my Patrick. I truly would have never made it through this without you. You are the most incredible spouse creature a weird witchy author could dream of. (It's me, I'm the weird witchy author.)

To my crones. You held my hand through more

versions of this book than I'd care to remember. Thank you for being both lifeboat and lighthouse as we navigate uneasy publishing seas.

To Jen Azantian and Olivia Valcarce, Ber's earliest and fiercest champions. Forever grateful and lucky to count you as both friends and colleagues.

To Erica Sussman, Briana Wood, and the entire team at Harper Children's. Books are complex beasts with many keepers; thank you for caring for Ber and me and all our collective demons with such thoughtfulness and brilliance.

And to everyone who supported the first book. For every diabetic, every friend of a diabetic, every reader who didn't know anything about diabetes before picking up this series and meeting my wild and wonderful diabetic witch. A book isn't finished until it is read. Thank you for finishing Ber's story with me, each and every one of you.